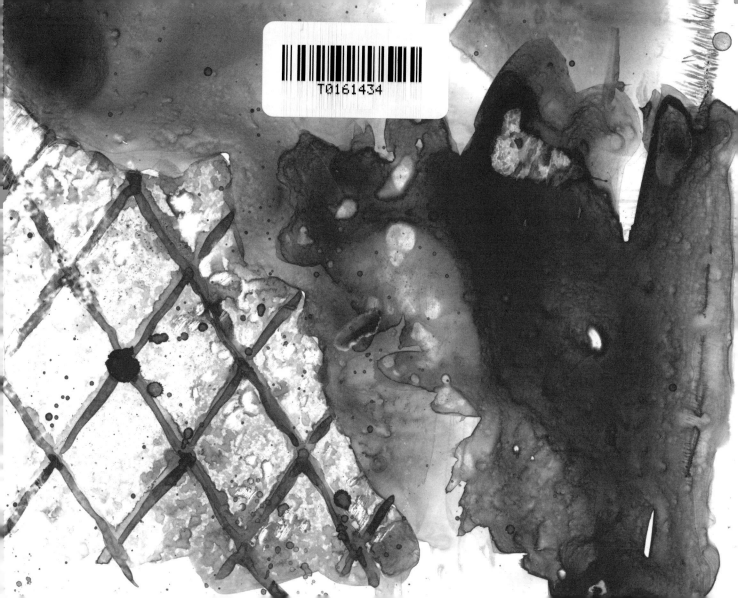

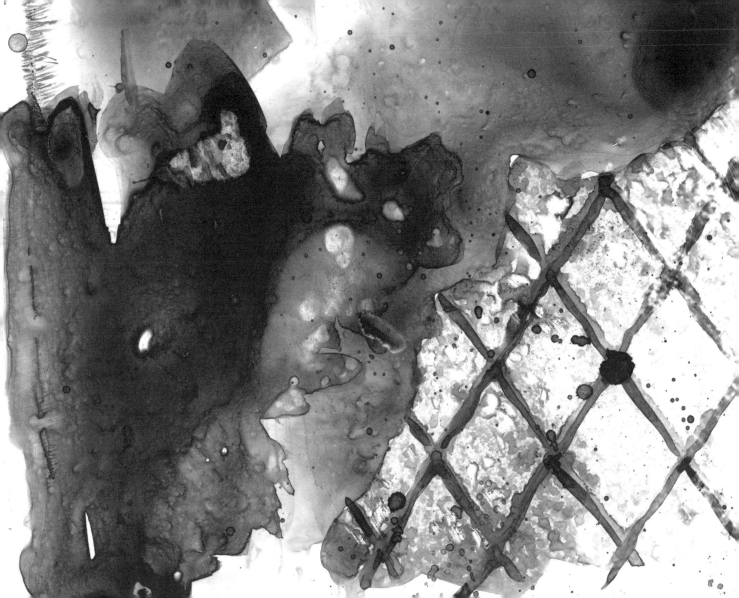

THE REASONABLE OGRE

The Reasonable Ogre

TALES FOR THE SICK AND WELL

Mike Barnes

ILLUSTRATIONS BY

Segbingway

BIBLIOASIS

FIRST EDITION

Library and Archives Canada Cataloguing in Publication

Barnes, Mike, 1955-
     The reasonable ogre : stories for the sick and well / Mike Barnes ; illustrator, Segbingway.

ISBN 978-1-926845-44-9

     I. Segbingway, 1974- II. Title.

PS8553.A7633R42 2012   C813'.54   C2011-907871-6

Biblioasis acknowledges the ongoing financial support of the Government of Canada through the Canada Council for the Arts, Canadian Heritage, the Canada Book Fund; and the Government of Ontario through the Ontario Arts Council.

PRINTED AND BOUND IN CANADA

To

Mary Margaret Barnes

and in memory of

William Henry Barnes M.D.

Contents

...hard bargains...

The Reasonable Ogre

Once there was an ogre who was like all other ogres except in one respect: he was reasonable. He could see more than one point of view, and he liked to argue and discuss. People seldom realized this, however, since he looked like any other ogre, huge and frightening, and he spent his time doing what every other ogre does: grabbing passersby and stuffing them in his mouth. He lived in a cave by a crossroads, where he slept away most of the day; but if he was awake and heard footsteps, he rushed out with a roar and planted himself in the roadway. No matter how loudly the person screamed (they always screamed), he snatched them up in his great hairy hand and ate them in two or three bites, cleaning his teeth afterward with branches he'd torn off trees.

One day a lawyer happened by. She was dressed very smartly, and the clicking of her heels woke the ogre up. He jumped into the roadway and confronted her. Instead of screaming she began talking quickly—not because she knew he was a reasonable ogre, but from the habits she'd learned in the courtroom.

"At least leave me my hair and eyes, since my husband says they are my best features," she reasoned with the ogre.

And the ogre, thinking he could make a very good meal without her hair and eyes, agreed.

"And leave me my hands, so I can do a little typing to earn my living," she said.

Again the ogre thought this was not too much to ask, and agreed.

"And my feet," she continued, "since everyone needs to have a little fun, and I love dancing."

Even without hair, hands, feet and eyes she is still a nice plump meal, thought the ogre, and nodded in agreement.

In this way the clever lawyer got the ogre to make an exception for one leg, then the other leg, then one arm, then the other arm, then her neck since how else would she hold her head up, then her heart since it would need to pump blood to whatever remained, and then—

"STOP!" bellowed the ogre. "You ask for too much! You are greedy, not reasonable."

The lawyer's mouth dropped open in astonishment. And then, before she could even scream, the ogre ate her in two great bites.

Now, during this debate, a young boy had been approaching the crossroads. He saw the lawyer get eaten despite her clever arguments. He wasn't clever at arguing, but he was a very fast runner, and he thought that might give him a chance.

The ogre towered over him, his mouth still bloody from his meal. He snatched up the boy and held him in front of his horrible face. "What do you have to say for yourself?" the ogre demanded.

"I have an interesting argument," said the boy. "If you put me down so I can catch my breath, I'll tell it to you."

"That is what everyone says who wants to run away," said the ogre, and stuffed the boy down his throat without even chewing.

Along came a poor man, a musician. He had been walking toward the crossroads and he saw what had happened to the lawyer and the boy. He was a humble man, used to life's hard bargains, so he thought he would try a different approach.

When the ogre planted himself in front of him and opened his huge mouth, the musician said, "I saw you make a meal of that lawyer and then have

the little boy for dessert. You can't still be hungry."

"I eat whether I'm hungry or not," said the ogre. "You don't know my nature."

"Well, then," said the musician, who knew all too well the nature of ogres, "if you must eat some of me, at least leave me the parts I can't do without."

"Which parts?" the ogre asked.

"I could spare you one leg," said the musician, "since I could get around with a crutch. But I need both of my hands to play my music."

"What instrument do you play?" asked the ogre.

"The harmonica."

"You don't need two hands for that," said the ogre. "One hand and a mouth are enough."

"That is true," said the honest musician. "Life would be more difficult, but I could manage."

"Since you are fair with me, I will be fair with you," said the reasonable ogre. "I will take one of your legs but just two fingers from your left hand."

And that is what the ogre did. And now the poor musician gets around with a crutch, and plays the harmonica and the recorder too. And when the talk turns to ogres, he tells people that though there is usually no reasoning with them, it never hurts to try.

Silver

A village beside a stream was slowly dying. Once it had been prosperous and happy, but now its children were becoming sick and families were moving away. No one knew the cause. One night an old man in the village dreamed of an ugly, ancient fish gasping at the bottom of a muddy pool. When he awoke he said to his wife, "Our water is the problem. I will follow the stream to its source and see what I find." His wife feared that she would never see him again, but she did not try to stop him. They had no children and they were old. Who else in the village could make the trip?

By the side of the stream they parted tearfully. "I'll come back," the old man promised. "But not before I've found what I'm looking for."

At first he had a pleasant walk. The stream wound through meadows and he walked beside it with his stick in the sun. But when the stream entered the forest, the way became more difficult. Often his path was blocked by a fallen tree, which he climbed over with difficulty, and the ground beside the stream became wet and muddy, so that his boots sank into it

and he had to pull them free with a sucking sound. It was hard to tell the slow-moving stream from the swamp around it.

At one difficult place he stopped to rest and eat a bit of bread, when he saw a little silver minnow having trouble like his own. The minnow was trying to swim up the stream but its way was blocked by a stick. The old man removed the stick, and smiled to see the minnow dart on with a flick of its tail.

Farther on, he saw the minnow stopped again, this time by a line of little stones and mud. The minnow swam up and down the line trying to find a place to get through. The old man reached down and with two fingers made a channel through the stones. With a flick of its tail, the silver minnow shot through.

I'll follow it, thought the old man. It knows where to go, and if it gets stuck I can help it. In this way the two made their way farther up the stream. The old man catching sight of a silver flash when he'd lost his way, and the minnow finding the way cleared when it had been blocked. They travelled for many days. The man's food was all gone, but the ground was dry

and the walking easier as he climbed beside the stream into the hills. The stream ran swift and clear, and made pools in level areas. Always, when he stopped beside one of these for the night, he would see the silver minnow glinting below, resting after the day's hard swimming.

Then, one day, the stream ran under a rock and disappeared. The silver minnow swam into the hole and was gone. The man walked carefully back and forth beyond the rock, but could find no sign of the stream returning to the surface. The ground was dry everywhere he looked. Tired and discouraged, he lay down to rest. His bones were aching and he groaned through a fitful sleep.

When he awoke, the sun was low. Peering at it from under his hand, he thought he saw a flash of silver farther up the hill. It could be the sun on a rock, or my mind playing tricks on me, he thought, but I've got to follow it and see.

But at the first step he took in the direction of the flash, a voice said firmly, *Give up what's precious or go no further.*

Startled, the old man looked all about him to see who had spoken, but there was no one there. The voice seemed to come from the trees and rocks and forest shadows.

He thought, I don't know what's precious, but I know what I need. I'll give up my walking stick. And as soon as he thought that, the walking stick disappeared. He looked around him, but it was gone. Far up the hill he saw the flash of silver again, and when he had reached it, limping slowly without his stick, he saw that it was the little stream, returned to the surface and catching the last light of the sun.

By now it was dark and he lay down for the night. When he got up to follow the stream again, he had only gone a short way before the voice stopped him:

Give up what's precious or go no further.

The old man thought. My food is gone, my stick is gone. I don't know what's precious but I know what I need. And no sooner had he thought of his clothes than they disappeared and he was naked.

Now he began to suffer badly. He limped painfully without his stick, and he shivered from the cold without clothes to protect him. Still, he made it a little farther along the stream before nightfall. There he spent a miserable night, shivering and groaning.

Again, the next morning, the voice stopped him before he had gone ten paces:

Give up what's precious or go no further.

The old man slumped down beside the stream. He began to cry. "What else can I give? I am hungry and

sore, tired, naked, and above all, old. I have nothing more."

Give up what's precious or go no further.

Closing his eyes, he smelled the fresh running water, and he put his aching feet in the cold stream to soothe them. I could find my way without eyes, he thought, and with the thought he was instantly blind. Day and night were the same to him now, and he stumbled up the stream in his bare feet, stopping only when he could not go another step without resting. He felt more hopeless but also more determined than ever, and when the voice spoke again, he was ready for it.

"Take my hands," he said back to it. "I don't need them to walk." And his hands fell at his sides, limp and useless.

Now he was without almost everything: a blind, handless, naked old man, limping slowly up a cold stream. All that filled his mind as he made his way haltingly on, was the thought of his village, slowly sickening and emptying of people, and of his wife, an old woman in a hut waiting for him to return.

Give up what's precious or go no further.

I can't give up my wife or my village, he thought. They're not mine to give. All I have is my memories of them. And with that his mind went completely blank, like a window wiped clean of dust.

Now he could only splash forward through the water following his nose, like a creature of instinct, not remembering the reason. He grew weak from hunger and cold. Finally he could go no further and he collapsed on a rock with his feet in the water, knowing he had reached the end. Though he could not see or know it, the stream had reached an end too. He was sitting beside its final pool, where the stream bubbled up from somewhere deep in the earth. In the clear water near his feet flashed the little silver fish, which had reached the pool long before.

Give up what's precious or go no further, said the voice, as sternly as ever despite the old man's state.

"I have nothing left to give," said the old man tiredly. "If it's nothing you want, then take it."

And with that he fell over, dead, into the pool and sank slowly to the bottom.

Far away, in the village he'd left behind, the old woman wondered what had happened to her husband. For days she had waited for him by the stream where they'd parted. Then she returned to their hut and waited some more, though with a smaller and smaller hope that he would ever return. Gradually, with a sinking heart, she accepted the fact that she would never see him again. One of the few young men left in the village offered to search for the old man. He followed the stream a long, long way, up to where it disappeared into the ground. There he found the old man's walking stick and his clothes. He brought these back and gave them to the old woman. Tears ran silently from her eyes at this proof that her husband had died.

Not only was he gone, but the sickness in the village was worse than ever. Families moved away until only a few remained, along with a scattering of old people. The stream they lived by behaved strangely that year. For weeks it dried up almost completely, shrinking to a trickle of murky, foul-tasting water. Then suddenly it gushed down and flooded over its banks, like water bursting through a dam, colder and clearer than before. The people shook their heads in puzzlement, since there had been neither drought nor heavy rains.

One day, a boy in the village went fishing and caught a plump silver fish. He was taking it home to his family for dinner, when he saw the old woman whose husband had disappeared, walking alone by the stream as she often did. Taking pity on her, he gave her the fish for her own dinner. The next morning, he knocked on her door to see how she'd enjoyed it. Getting no answer, he pushed the door open. Inside the hut he saw a beautiful young woman in a green dress lying on a bed. On a plate on the wooden

table were the bones of the fish, stripped clean of meat. He went to the bed and touched her hand, which was as cold as ice.

He ran to get his parents, who returned with some of the village elders. The oldest of these said the dead woman on the bed was the old woman as she had looked sixty years before, on her wedding day.

After that, the remaining young families moved away, more certain than ever that their village was cursed. Those who were too old to move died one by one, and soon the village was deserted, its huts collapsing into grass. Which was a shame, because at last the water in the stream was perfectly clean and safe for anyone to drink.

Moonswoop

When she was very young, Moira got so sick that she had to stay inside for a whole year. Her mom made up her bed beside the living-room window, and Moira sat with a pillow behind her back, colouring pictures and watching the seasons slowly change beyond the glass. Their apartment was on the fourth floor, and when she leaned her forehead on the glass, she could see the tops of people's heads going by in the street below. A tall maple tree stood outside the window, and behind it clouds passed slowly, and planes a little more quickly. Little birds landed in the tree and flitted from branch to branch. Sometimes they all stopped moving at once, then dropped straight down like stones falling, and Moira knew that the hawk was nearby. She would see the hawk floating in a circle high above, or diving down into her tree or another, its wings pinned close to its sides. It sailed past her window with its ragged wings rippling like old flags, sometimes with another, identical hawk following close behind, like a twin sister or a reflection in a mirror of air. Once it sat for a few minutes on a branch just beyond the window, and

Moira memorized it to draw later: black, curved talons digging into bark; gray-white, tawny-yellow and brown feathers; the beak like a short, thick hook bent downwards.

In November, when she had been inside for half a year, Moira began to grow wings of her own. She felt them first as hard knots in her shoulders. She couldn't get comfortable lying on her back, and when she felt behind her, her hands touched little hard mounds like buds below her shoulder blades, with a covering of first feathers so fine they felt like fur. Within a few days, the wings had grown long enough to tickle the small of her back with their tips. She used new muscles to make them twitch—she just thought about it and it happened—though of course she couldn't unfold them inside the apartment. For now she kept them tucked under her nightgown, pinned as flat against her body as she could make them, and was careful not to say a word about them to her mom.

One night she waited until her mom was asleep and then opened her window and crawled out on the ledge of their building. She had unbuttoned the back of her nightgown, and now she felt the wings unfold behind her and rise and stretch out in the cold night air. They swept downward slowly and she felt her feet leave the ledge for a moment. She flapped them again, more vigorously, and the next thing she knew, she was standing on a branch at the top of the maple tree, already above the roof of her building. To get the feel of her new wings, she flew in a wide circle over her neighbourhood. She found the air currents that allowed her to float, barely moving her wings, like a boat on a lazy river. Then she flew much higher, circling the city on the river of air, looking down at the thousands of twinkling lights, behind which people slept or dreamed or read books by bedside lamps. She tried to pick out her home, but from high above, many houses and buildings looked alike.

She looked above her and saw the moon, full and shining white. Banking like an airplane, she steered toward it, flapping hard and with a steady rhythm.

She flew without stopping for a night and a day and another night. The moon ahead grew larger and larger, until it filled the sky and she could see nothing else. And then she was at it—at the moon—flying above its gray dust and black craters. The sky was not blue, of course, but she could breathe the air, which was very cold and had a faintly sweet taste, a bit like peppermint on a winter's day. Why had no one ever told her that you could breathe on the moon? And why had they always said that no one lived there—when she could see now tiny dots of light in the craters below? True, they weren't very bright, not even as bright as candles, but there seemed to be as many of them as she had seen above her city on earth. Most of them were in the deepest craters, with only a few in the smaller craters and none at all on the surface. After flying around the whole moon once, she aimed herself toward the largest, blackest, deepest crater and flew in slowly narrowing circles down into it.

As she descended, she saw the little lights wink out one by one. At the bottom of the crater was a faint pearly glow, a milky gray, and in this half-light she saw the small bunched shapes of people gathered beneath her. When she got closer she saw children with upturned faces and raised arms pointing at her. She swooped lower, and they scattered as if at a signal, running into holes like caves and into the deep black shadows behind rocks.

She landed on the soft gray dust, her wings stirring up small puffs of it. It felt strange to stand again after such a long flight. Her wings settled down along her back, sliding and tucking close like fans folding up. She saw that the soft gray light came from the moon's dust,

which from up close had a low pulsing glow, like a candle flickering in slow motion. The milky light hovered near the surface, a fuzzy gray quilt pulled up over ancient rock and dust. Above that was the deep black velvet of space, with the faraway earth shining in it like a blue-and-white streaked marble. The moon's air was cold but not freezing. And absolutely still, without any wind at all. As Moira stood there, with her toes curling into the soft old dust, she felt the eyes, many pairs of them, watching her from the black shadows.

At last, a tall, thin shape came out from behind a rock and walked toward her. It was a boy, a few years older than Moira. He was very tall and terribly thin, so thin that Moira thought he must almost disappear when he turned sideways. He had yellow hair, dark sad eyes, and silvery skin. His skin was the dull gleaming gray of the mercury in her mom's old thermometer. His name, he said, was Edgewick. He was the oldest child on the moon.

Now the other moon children approached from all sides, the littlest ones holding hands as if they were crossing a busy street. They stood in a circle watching Moira closely. They all had Edgewick's solemn, dark eyes and silvery skin. Finally, two of the smallest children, a boy and a girl, walked over to Moira and asked if she was hungry. A little, she answered, and they led

her, each taking one of her hands, across the bottom of the crater to a cave that became a tunnel that led downward deeper into the moon.

At the bottom of the tunnel was a cavern they called the Jampot. It was huge, bigger than a church, and filled with a softly shining white light, like the glow from a giant flashlight inside an enormous tent. It was the light, Edgewick told her, that made the milky glow above, seeping up through cracks and tiny holes in the crater. The floor of the Jampot was spongy; with each step, Moira's feet sank into it a little, as if she were walking on marshmallows. The children led her to the wall and showed her how to break off a piece with her fingers. They nibbled at the edges of it, and so did Moira; it tasted sweet but dry, like a cross between angel food cake and stale white bread. All around the huge space children were taking little handfuls of the wall and nibbling on them. Each handful made the cavern a wee bit larger, hollowing it out a little bit more. After a first bite, most of the children took their piece to a pool bubbling in the centre of the room. It was filled with a thick, bright red liquid that looked like jam thickening on the stove. But when Moira dipped her piece into the sticky red, she found it was cold, and all she could taste was sweetness, like red syrup. Jamcake, the children

called the bready handfuls dipped in the syrup. It was the only food on the moon.

Moira felt full after only a few mouthfuls, and she noticed that none of the children ate very much. Edgewick didn't eat at all, which told her how he had got so thin. After the snack, they lay around on the soft floor, which was, Edgewick told her, made of the same stuff as the walls, but dirty and packed down by people walking on it. Everyone resting after eating reminded Moira of quiet time after milk and cookies, except that these were the most serious, well-behaved children she had ever seen. They seldom spoke, and when they did it was in hushed voices. Someone might smile, a little sadly, but there was no laughing or joking. There had been no running or pushing on the way down the tunnel.

"Why are they all staring at me?" she asked Edgewick. Wherever she looked, she met another pair of eyes watching her intently.

"They're wondering when you'll start to take them back," Edgewick answered.

"Me!" Moira said in surprise. "How did they get here in the first place?"

Edgewick looked away, and his voice when he answered sounded sadder and more solemn than ever. "Everyone comes here the same way," he said.

If that is the case, Moira wondered, why do they need my help to get back? But before she could ask Edgewick, her two guides came to show her something else. All around the sides of the Jampot cavern, children were disappearing into small round shadows that Moira guessed were the entrances to other, smaller tunnels. She went down one of these now with the children, followed by Edgewick. In places the tunnel crossed other tunnels, and looking down these, Moira saw other children walking, sometimes disappearing suddenly as they turned down another passageway. Each child seemed to have its own route, and she wondered why the boy and girl leading her were always—

"Twins," Edgewick whispered from behind her, as if he could read her thoughts.

The tunnel they were in got gradually smaller, so that Moira's shoulders brushed the sides and she and Edgewick had to duck their heads. Just when it seemed that it might close up completely, it opened into a room, a snug, nest-like chamber that was obviously the twins' home. A little round window in the opposite wall glowed with a pale blue light. In front of it was a ledge of rock, like a bench, and the twins motioned for Moira to sit down on it. When she did, she saw, so clearly that it made her start, a small Chinese woman hanging a checkered shirt on a clothesline. She reached down to get another shirt from a hamper on the ground, picking up two more clothespins from a basket beside it. She was small because she was far away, but still Moira could see the lines in her neck when she turned her face up into the breeze that made the clothes sway. She took a few steps across her yard to a tree that was beginning to flower. Moira saw the pinkish blossoms so clearly she could almost smell them. The window seemed to follow the woman like a camera, and when she put the empty basket on her hip and turned to go into her house, pausing to examine a potted plant by the door, Moira felt the twins nudging her to get up. They slipped behind her and sat close together on the little bench, watching in complete absorption as the pale blue light rippled over their faces.

Edgewick tugged at Moira's sleeve, and they left the room and walked up the long tunnel until they were again on the floor of the crater where Moira had landed. There Edgewick told Moira about the window and what she'd seen in it.

The pale blue light was earthlight, he explained. The earth reflected sunlight back to the moon, just as people on the earth saw reflected light they called moonlight. The little round window was the eyepiece of a long, long telescope that went all the way out to the surface. Each child on the moon watched one person's life on earth.

"Just one?" Moira asked.

"Only one," Edgewick answered.

Moira thought of all the people she saw on the street below her window, and the millions and millions of other people going about their lives. One was a better number than nothing, but it was still a very small number.

"How can anyone pick just one?" she asked.

Edgewick shrugged. "In the end you just do," he said.

He showed her to a room that was empty, and Moira began living her life on the moon. When she was hungry she walked down the tunnels to the Jampot and ate some Jamcake. She pulled a little piece from the sweet white wall and dipped it into the bubbling red. Other children lay around the Jampot floor, but after the first few days, the older ones stopped watching her closely. Even the little ones paid less attention, glancing over whenever she came in but then seeming to get bored and looking away. In her room she sat in front of her telescope and watched little scenes from the lives of people on earth. A boy tying his shoelaces, an old man reading a newspaper on a bench in a park, a well-dressed woman getting on an elevator. Each view lasted only a few seconds and then switched to another, like a television running

rapidly through its channels. Moira understood now why eventually you had to pick one person. It was better to have one full meal every day than a hundred tiny bites. When she got tired of the constantly changing views, she climbed up the long tunnel to walk on the floor of the crater.

Edgewick was always there, walking through the milky glow that came from the slowly hollowing Jampot far below them. As they walked together, Moira occasionally saw glints of light from the steep walls of the crater. The angle had to be just right to see one, and it flashed like a signal and then was gone. These puzzled her at first, until she realized that they were bits of earthlight flashing from the lenses of the telescopes trained on earth. Those were the lights, the lights of a city of moon children, she had seen as she flew over the crater. All of the children stayed below, eating Jamcake and watching through their telescopes, and Edgewick was the only person she ever met on the surface. One day she asked him why.

"The others will come out for a landing. Like they did with you," he said. "But once they start watching an Otherone, they don't like to leave for too long."

"You leave," Moira said. "Don't you like to watch?"

"I don't need to," said Edgewick, and looked away quickly as if he was embarrassed.

After a few days on the moon, Moira felt that it might be time to fly back home. She liked Edgewick, and she liked being able to walk about and see other children instead of staying by herself in bed—but she missed her mom, and she even missed the tops of people's heads and the birds hopping among the maple leaves beyond her window. She still hadn't picked an Otherone to watch. She was afraid that if she did, she would never see her mom again. Edgewick seemed so sad and lonely that she thought it was better not to say goodbye to him. Up on the surface, she unfolded her wings and flapped them once, hard. Nothing happened. She flapped them quickly, so quickly she felt a pain like fire in her shoulders; this time she rose a few inches and bobbed unevenly along, but she had to beat her wings wildly, and the moment she stopped, she plopped back down in the dust.

Edgewick found her sitting on a rock with her face in her hands, crying.

"They won't work here," he explained when she had calmed down enough to listen. "Your wings, I mean. After a while, they get small. They get weak. Then . . . they go away completely. They disappear."

"But you said the others were waiting for me to take them back. Why would they think that?" Moira asked.

Edgewick gave one of his slow, sad shrugs. "The little ones forget. They can't remember how they got here. They think a hawk brought them. They have nightmares about bad hawks snatching them from their rooms, and they have good dreams of friendly hawks taking them back."

"And the older ones?"

"They just hope. Without knowing any more what they're hoping for. Nothing lasts very long with them . . . not even hope. They just get used to eating their Jamcake and watching their Otherone."

"But not you," Moira said. "You're up here walking. Why aren't you down below with the others, watching?"

Edgewick looked embarrassed again at the question. "I told you, I don't need to," he said quickly. "And I can't now, anyway."

Moira was still confused, but she was too upset about her own shrinking wings to question Edgewick further. When she tried to fly the next day, she jumped up high, once, like someone taking a first jump on a trampoline, but then dropped back to the moon and couldn't leave it again, no matter how hard she flapped. When she reached around behind her, she felt the wings getting smaller, drawing back into her shoulders the same way they had emerged. She felt so miserable that for two days after that she didn't leave her room, not even to get Jamcake. She was faint with hunger when she went up to the surface again. Edgewick was there, walking in his slow, thoughtful manner.

"How can you stand it?" she asked, after telling him of the pains in her stomach from not eating for two days. "I've never seen you eat a thing," she said. "Don't you ever get hungry?"

"I'm hungry all the time," Edgewick said.

"But you never eat?"

"As little as possible," he said. "I starve and starve . . . and then, when I can't stand it anymore . . . I take a tiny bite."

"But why?" she asked.

Edgewick didn't answer right away. He looked up out of the crater, up at the blue-white marble planet floating in the black sky, and then back down at Moira. "It's an experiment," he said. And then paused again, as if deciding whether he should say more. "I'll tell you if you promise not to tell anyone else."

"I promise," Moira said.

"All right. Flap your wings."

"What?" She shook her head; she'd had enough of that sadness. But Edgewick insisted, "Flap your wings," and so, reluctantly, she did. She arced up into the air and hung high above Edgewick, who in his thinness looked like a flagpole planted in a pool of pale pulsing light. She started to circle, but then felt suddenly tired, and cruised in a tight spiral back to the ground. When she had got her breath back, Edgewick explained.

"It's the Jamcake," he said. "Something about the food here . . . as soon as you start eating it, you have to stay. I don't think anyone else knows. They just think they lost their wings. Or they forget they ever had them. I didn't know for a long time. And then I stopped eating and found out. By accident, like you."

"So you can fly again?" Moira said excitedly.

Edgewick looked as if she had just slapped him. He looked too sad even to cry; otherwise, Moira thought, he would be spilling buckets now.

"It might be too late," he said quietly. "I think I waited too long. Here, see for yourself." He turned around and lifted up the back of his shirt. Moira saw two small, blackish mounds, like stumps with scabs, with a few limp feathers hanging from them. They looked like the remains of wings she'd seen on dead birds lying by the side of the road.

"They're growing," she lied. "You'll get them back."

Edgewick shook his head. "No, not now. At first I thought so. I could jump up, and even glide a bit. But it

didn't last. They shrank back. After a while it gets permanent."

"But you're still not eating," she said.

"No," he said dully, "I'm not." They walked for a while in silence, sometimes crossing the trails they'd left on other walks, their footprints clear as photographs since nothing disappeared on the windless moon.

"Listen," Edgewick said suddenly, with a brightness in his voice Moira had never heard before, as if, just now, he'd finally found something worth saying. "It may not be too late yet for you. Let's do another experiment. Let's try."

Moira agreed. Part of her wanted nothing more than to stay on the moon, walking through the chilly pools of light with Edgewick, nibbling Jamcake and watching some Otherone live a life on earth. But with another part she longed to flap with the strongest wings she could find back to her own life on earth, even if it was just to sit in her bed, watching through her window and colouring pictures and listening to her mom hum along with the radio while she cooked their dinner.

For the next few days she didn't eat a thing. Her stomach grumbled and cramped terribly, and all she could think about was food. But then the worst cramps passed and she felt mainly empty in her middle and weak and easily tired. Pictures of food came into her head constantly, but often they made her feel a little sick. She was getting out of the habit of eating, Edgewick said. They walked together on the surface every day, stopping every few steps to let Moira rest. Walking made the wings grow faster, Edgewick told her, and it kept you away from Jamcake and the sight of other children eating. Sometimes she felt faint and dizzy, her head spinning from hunger, but she also felt the stirrings again of the muscles around her shoulders, the wings bunching and twitching there like colts desperate to run, even as the rest of her body got weaker and weaker. The blue-white marble in the black above looked different now that she hoped to visit it again. She couldn't say how exactly. But it was like a dot on a map you plan to travel to, which, once you know you will visit it, goes from being a dot like any other dot to a dot that is really a city filled with streets and people and new things to see and do. Of course, she didn't mention that to Edgewick, who seldom looked at the earth, but whenever he did, looked sadder than ever.

After two weeks of not eating, she was too weak to walk and had to stay on the ledge in her room. She lay with her back to the little blue window, which made her head spin with its quickly changing scenes. Each day she didn't eat, she scratched a mark on the rock above the bench. There were fifteen lines scratched there now. Edgewick came every day to visit her. This was the tricky time, he told her. Her wings might not be strong enough yet, but if she didn't leave now, she would have to start eating a little, just to stay alive. Little nibbles of Jamcake would keep her going, but would also slow down her wings. Everything would happen much more slowly, Edgewick said.

Moira knew she had to try. She couldn't wait any longer.

It was strange to leave a place without packing or saying goodbye. But she had brought nothing with her, so she had nothing to take back. And though she had talked to the other moon children when she met them in the tunnels or around the Jampot, she found it hard to remember their names or what they had talked about. It was hard even to remember their faces. With their silvery skin and dark eyes like coals, they all looked much the same. There was only Edgewick to say goodbye to. They stood on the floor of the crater, with the foggy glowing light around their feet and the moon's black sky above them.

"I'll miss you," Moira said. "You won't have anyone to talk to."

"That's true," Edgewick nodded sadly. "But I'll have someone to watch again."

And Moira understood, at last, what she should have guessed before. Why, from the moment she arrived, Edgewick had had nothing to do except walk on the floor of the crater and wait for her to walk and talk with him.

"Goodbye," Moira said.

"Goodbye," said Edgewick. "Fly hard."

Moira turned and walked a few paces away. She unfolded her wings and felt them rise above her back. They felt as strong, or almost, as they had back on her window ledge. She turned to look one last time at Edgewick, memorizing his yellow hair and mercury skin. He made an "Up, up!" motion with his hands. He was telling her to go . . . go . . . go. She flapped once, to clear the ground, then twice more, three times, hard. She was high above Edgewick now. He looked like a flagpole or a tall, bare tree. She was halfway up the walls of the deep crater. Before she left, she made one slow gliding circle. Now, around the bare stick that was Edgewick, she saw dots as the other children gathered, their pale upturned faces shining like mushrooms. It was flight that drew them out, someone coming or going. Only that could tempt them from the Otherones in the flickering earthlight of their telescopes. As she began to climb higher, they left by ones and twos, disappearing like ants back into their shadows and tunnels. Only Edgewick remained, unmoving, watching faithfully.

She climbed in a spiral the walls of the crater, just as she had come down them, and then began the long flapping journey across space back to earth. Her second wings were not as strong and it took her much longer, many days and nights of hard flying. Earthlight grew stronger until it was a blue lake of light she was swimming through. Earth's huge coloured continents and oceans filled her sight until the gray and black moon behind her seemed tiny, almost a dream. Her country loomed . . . then her city, her street, her building . . . and then her window, still open partway, as if waiting for her to return. Her bed was made up and the covers turned down for her. She slipped into it quietly, anxious to see her mom again but glad to have some time by herself to get used to being back. For now she felt herself to be not quite a moon child, not quite an earth child—but a hawk that flapped in blackness somewhere between the two.

In the morning would be her reunion with her mom, and the happy tears they would shed together. And many questions—Where did you go? Why did you stay away so long?—that Moira wouldn't be able

[44]

to answer. No one on the moon had told her that the life there was a secret, but she felt somehow it was. And besides, no one would understand or even believe that other world who hadn't been there. And if they had been there, there was nothing she needed to say.

She got better, but very slowly. It was many more months before she could go outside, and more months after that before she could return to school. She was older than the other children in her class, who kept their distance from her, as if they sensed she had been to a strange place and might be somehow dangerous. Moira didn't mind. She liked being by herself. Her wings were gone now. She had only two small sore places, like tender bruises, where they'd been. It had started happening as soon as she got back, even though she wasn't eating Jamcake or anything like it. Moira knew, a little sadly, that they would never return. And that she would never tell anyone the whole truth about where she'd been. No one would ever know that when she looked up at the moon, she saw more than a white shining disc in the sky.

Sometimes in art class she drew pictures of craters and tunnels and children with silver skin and a boy so tall and thin the other children said he must be a skeleton. Good, good, very interesting, said the art teacher, but the way he said it told Moira that her pictures were not good or interesting, or not in the right way at least, and she went back to drawing what the other children were drawing: houses with chimneys with smoke curling out of them, clouds, trees, and a yellow sun. She did well in art and English and music, and not quite so well in math and gym. At home or in school, she tried to do everything as well as she could, so that Edgewick would have a good life to watch from the moon.

The Jailed Wizards

A wizard caught a rival wizard and locked him in a dungeon beneath his castle. First he stripped the captive of all his magical powers. Then he left him in a small, bare room, cold and damp and almost completely dark except for a bit of grayish light that leaked through a tiny barred window high above the floor. The stone walls were so thick that the imprisoned wizards—who were numerous, for the powerful wizard made war on anyone whose magic he felt threatened his own—could not even hear each other's screams.

"How long will you keep me here?" the prisoner asked before his captor shut the stone door.

"How long does a wizard live?"

"Forever," said the prisoner.

"That is how long you will remain," said the powerful wizard. And he closed the massive door with a crash, and sealed it with an unbreakable spell.

Years passed. Twice a day a slot beside the door clanked open. The first time, a dirty hand pushed through a lump of stale bread and a cup of water; later, another dirty hand took back the cup. Nothing else occurred. Until one day the massive door creaked open on its ancient hinges, and the powerful wizard stood before his former rival, now filthy and wretched and listless with despair. "I have decided *forever* is the wrong sentence for you," he announced. "There is a crack in the wall that lengthens a little each year. I am sure you have studied it. When it reaches the floor, I will let you go."

"I thank you," mumbled the prisoner.

"Don't," said the wizard. "This is not mercy. I want you to suffer as much as possible. Those who lose all hope do not suffer like those who still believe their suffering may one day end. That is all. Goodbye."

Years passed again, but now they passed with the constant measuring of a tiny crack. Many times a day, the jailed wizard reached up and ran his hand over the break in the stone, wondering if it had lengthened by a hair or if he was only imagining that. It did, in fact, grow longer, but it did so with horrible slowness. Once, he did not allow himself to measure the crack for a hundred days—two hundred openings and closings of the slot—and when he measured it again, he was sure it was a finger's width closer to the floor. Ten years passed in this way. Then twenty years. Then thirty. Now the crack in the wall had reached the level of his eyes. Now, he thought, I know I will get out one day. But when? In five hundred years? A thousand? I mustn't think of that. One day I'll leave.

Many long years later, the jailed wizard was standing next to the wall where he spent his days, examining the crack with his eyes and fingers to see if it had changed, when he was startled by a tiny movement just above him. Something very small and dark was moving within the crack. As the wizard watched, an ant stuck its head out of the crack, its tiny antennae moving in the stale air. Tears filled the wizard's eyes to find his absolute loneliness broken by a visit from another creature, even an ant. Tears of joy and misery ran down his wrinkled face and into his long, dirty beard. Despite his extreme hunger, in the coming days he put little pellets of bread in the crack, and soon he had a line of ants he could watch, coming to get his crumbs and carrying them along the crack and out the window back to their nest. The sight brought joy and endless interest, and it stirred guilty memories.

Long ago, in one of the endless wars that are a wizard's life, he had defeated a very minor wizard. The defeated wizard had been a storyteller, which is one of the lowest and most common grades of magic. Cruelly, out of sheer contempt, the victorious wizard had taken the defeated wizard's strength and long life, though he had left him, as a power not worth stealing, his storytelling art. Now the jailed wizard struggled to remember what he had once known of this lesser magic. A story was at least a way of reaching other ears. This, after freedom, was what he longed for most.

Tiny animals, he remembered, were often used to gather stories and return them to the storyteller. Since the animals couldn't speak our language, people told them things they would tell no other person, secure in the knowledge they could not repeat it. He couldn't remember exactly how it was done, but even without a wizard's magic he still had a wizard's cunning, and he invented a way. He placed a tiny pellet of bread inside his ear and stood with his ear against the crack. Soon he felt the tickle of an ant entering his ear. He turned from the wall and plugged his ear with his finger. He felt the ant touch his finger and then, finding no way out, turn the other way and explore the inner chambers of his ear, walking around the words of the story in his head. When he judged that enough time had passed, he unplugged his ear and stood with his ear against the crack and let the ant find its way out. He watched it carry the pellet of bread and his story away up the crack toward

the window high above. Would it carry it to someone who could understand? Would it be crushed under a careless foot? Perhaps he would need to tell a thousand stories to a thousand ants before one would find a listening ear. He could do that. Before his imprisonment he had lived a long, eventful life, each day of which had teemed with stories. Sitting with his back against the stone wall, he began to prepare the next one.

Some weeks later, in the village near the powerful wizard's castle, an old, sick storyteller was sitting, as he always did, by the window of his hut. A line of bread crumbs and sugar led from his window to a stone covered with black ink, and beyond that to a sheet of clean white paper. The storyteller no longer had the strength to make up stories on his own, and he lived in the shrinking hope that one would come to him by itself. Day by day, ants walked over his trail of sugar crumbs and over his ink and paper. But the marks they made with their tiny inky feet spelled chaos, spelled nonsense—spelled nothing. Still, he had always done all he could do, and all he could do now was wait.

On this day, an ant came in across the window sill, walked down over his ink stone, and across his paper. Around it went in a circle—**O**—and then down, and up, and across a short curve, and down again—**n**. **O** . . . **n** . . . **c** . . . **e**—"Once," the storyteller murmured with excitement, "once . . . and then?" Gently he sprinkled more sugar crumbs on the page, and waited, while the ant waved its antennae, and continued tracing letters with its feet.

I knew, I knew, I knew, whispered the storyteller. I knew there was no better place to wait than near a castle filled with jailed wizards, souls with endless tales to tell and no one but the ants to tell them to.

...small plenties...

Neverday: The Grateful Sprites

You will find on Saturday
You on Friday next
You will dig till Neverday
And then you'll find what's best

*I*n a village by the sea, a fisherman made a hard but happy living from his nets and boat. Often he came home empty-handed after a long day of setting and hauling, but he was young and strong and did not become discouraged for long. He remembered the other kind of day that came every so often, when fish of every kind slid into his boat and piled up flopping around his knees. On such days, after he had sold his catch at the market and given his parents what they needed for the house, he put whatever coins he had left in a wooden savings box he had carved. He loved a girl who worked in the fish market, and they planned to marry when the box was full. Her initials were cut into the bottom of the box, where he could feel them with his fingers whenever he counted his savings.

One day, he hauled up a strange fish in his net. Large and bright green, it lay quivering on its side, with one eye staring at him, under a pile of flipping and squirming herring. When he had removed the herring, he saw that a strand of the net was caught under the green fish's gill, with other strands wound tightly around its tail. As he moved to free it, the fish began speaking to him. Its lips moved only a little, but the voice, though quiet, was clear and high. I am a water sprite, said the green fish, put here under a spell. If you help me you will receive treasure more than you have ever wished for.

With or without the offer of reward, the fisherman was glad to help, and did as the green fish told him.

With his filleting knife, he scraped a green scale from the fish's side. Then a few salt crystals drying on the fish's spiny dorsal fin. Now you must take a drop of my blood, said the green fish. The fisherman hesitated; though he cut up fish every day, he had no wish to hurt this one. Go ahead, said the clear high voice. So the fisherman stuck the point of his knife into the fish's thick back muscle, where it would bleed but strike nothing vital. A bead of red blood stood on the point. Now take a piece of flesh from my belly. Again the

fisherman hesitated, but did as he was told. He cut a little wedge out of the fish's orange-yellow belly.

Now put those things in your left hand, and free me, said the fish.

The fisherman did as he was told. Green scale, salt crystals, drop of blood, and wedge of flesh went into his left hand, and he closed his fist over it, and with his right hand freed the green fish's gill and tail. As soon as he lifted the last strand, the fish was gone and a shining slender boy, draped in seaweed, stood in his boat.

The fisherman stepped back in shock, and heard a small clattering in the bottom of the boat. Looking down, he saw the jewels that had fallen from his open hand. He picked them up wonderingly: an emerald, three small pearls, a ruby, and a gold coin. He looked up at the slender boy with his glowing milky skin.

His pale green eyes had a mischievous twinkle, though he did not smile. They are yours to keep, he said, but if you bury them in a chest and wait a year, you will have more treasure than you have ever hoped for.

With that, the boy leapt nimbly into the water, and the astonished fisherman watched as a long milky shape sped quickly into the depths and out of sight.

That afternoon, on a pebbly beach beside the fish market, he and his beloved made their future plans excitedly. Though neither of them could judge the true worth of the jewels the fisherman now carried in a little bag hung inside his shirt, they knew that in a single miraculous encounter he had more than filled his savings box. They could marry now. Except—was it better to wait? What of the sprite's promise of even greater treasure if the jewels were buried in a chest for a year? They debated the question—spend what they had, or wait while it grew—each taking one side and then the other.

At last, however, the fisherman pointed out with a laugh that there was a middle way—obvious, yet they hadn't seen it. Bury the chest for a year, get married in the meantime; and if in a year it gave back only what they had now, why that was already more than they needed. She fretted that the sprite might trick them somehow, but he told her not to worry; why would the creature he had rescued want to trick him? Kissing him lightly, she agreed.

A year later to the day, he went alone to the small, unvisited beach, far from the village, where he had buried the chest. He had done so at night, using no light but the moon, and had carefully covered his traces. For the first week he had returned every night with his heart pounding, but never had he seen the slightest sign of any disturbance. He had stopped going, and had devoted himself to the happy duties of making a

home with his new wife. Now, returning to the beach, he was relieved to see sprigs of wiry grass growing in the sand above the chest, a sure sign that no one had found his hiding place.

He dug quickly with the spade he had brought. When he struck something with a hollow clunk, his heart skipped with excitement. Hurriedly he scraped away the sand. Without bothering to raise the box from the hole, he unlocked it and flung open the top.

It was empty. Not even the scattering of original jewels lay in it. He blinked rapidly in disbelief. Though it lay in shadow, the bare wood of the box's interior seemed to strike his eyes with a painful glare. Numbly, he groped inside the box, praying his fingers would find what his eyes had somehow missed. The cool wood felt like mockery. He remembered the sprite's pale laughing eyes. And wished with a trembling rage he'd gutted the green fish and tossed its filthy insides to the gulls.

With a hoarse shout of anger, he hurled the deceiving chest as far as he could and watched as the tide slowly moved it out to sea, wishing he had smashed holes in its bottom so that it would sink out of sight forever.

As he trudged home, he wondered how he would tell his wife the news. The fishing had been poor the past year, and it was only thanks to the little she made at the market, plus the occasional fish she was allowed to bring home, that they kept food on the table. Whenever things got too scanty, one or the other would say: Wait until the end of the year. Then our troubles will be gone for good. He paused on the road outside their small, unpainted hut.

Suddenly, the door sprang open and she ran down the path towards him. Had she seen him through the window and guessed from his face what had happened? Would she forget what they had both decided and blame him for their loss?

But, no; she was smiling. There was a wild light in her eyes. Here, she said, putting his hand on her belly. I am carrying our child.

THE BOY BORN nine months later was weak and sickly. A disease that wasted his muscles caused him to develop slowly and walk, when he eventually did, with difficulty. But despite this he was a happy child, meeting the world with a gurgling smile, and he soon became the joy of his parents' lives. His father stopped worrying so much about his fisherman's luck and simply accepted with a shrug what fortune the sea brought him: a fat fish for the table some days, with extra left for salting; nothing but his wife's coarse bread on others. In time he taught his son, who was too frail for an open boat, how to mend nets, sharpen knives and gaffs, caulk cracks, stitch sails, tend the vegetable patch behind their hut, and help with all the other jobs around the docks and house that didn't require strong legs and a steady gait. The boy learned everything quickly, and was a great help to both his mother and his father. Rowing back into the bay after a long day's fishing, the father felt his heart leap up in gladness when he turned and saw his son sitting on the dock waiting for him, the smoke curling from their hut behind him, where his wife always had vegetable soup simmering, as she considered it unlucky to count on fish no matter how good the sea had been to them lately.

Life offered them its small plenties, including, two years later, another son. From the start, this boy was as different from their first son as it was possible to be. His body was strong and his will was fierce; not only was he determined to go just where he wanted, but where he wanted to go was always the very place that others had ordered him to avoid. The fact that he grew up to be quick-witted and handsome only made him more difficult; whatever trouble his muscles and short temper spared him, his charm and cunning supplied. By fourteen, he was done with the village school and it was done with him; and the same could be said of the village girls: he had already broken the hearts of the prettiest, and their brothers and fathers were his sworn enemies. Having used up his life in the village, and restless to see the world, he slipped away one night with two other boys who were on the same reckless path.

Not surprisingly—for the sea soaked into every villager's pores, so that no one's living was unconnected with it—they became pirates. Though barely more than boys, they lived the thrilling life of robbers at sea, chasing or being chased over crashing waves, hunting down plump ships and fighting those on board to take whatever they carried. After only a few years serving under others, they took command of their own vessel. The fisherman's son became the captain, and his two village friends his trusted mates. They made a great deal of money but never became rich, as they gave generous shares to the sailors on their ship, and spent whatever was left on lavish parties for themselves and their friends. It was a fine, dangerous life, but they realized it could not go on forever. Already they had seen many of their pirate friends killed or captured. So the three friends made a pact to begin saving a part of what they stole, and to quit piracy forever when they had filled three chests

with treasure. Each would take his treasure chest and begin a new, honest life.

They kept their word to themselves. Pieces of gold and silver, rings and necklaces and bracelets taken from gentlemen and their ladies, soon covered, like a glittering mat, the bottom of the casket each kept under lock and key in his quarters.

One hot and windless day in the tropics, they came upon a merchant ship that they had been chasing for months without success. Though the ship was squat and laden with heavy cargo, it had a mysterious ability to outrun their own sleek vessel, tacking always just ahead of them on whatever sliver of wind could be found. Now, however, there was no wind to find an advantage with and the ship lay ahead of them, utterly becalmed. The pirates rowed over to seize it, the men shouting and brandishing their swords and pistols. They knew that such a show of force would often decide a battle beforehand, making bloodshed unnecessary. Indeed, when they boarded the becalmed merchant ship, its sailors already had trunks of valuables standing ready on the upper deck, and were bringing more up from below. An older sailor directing this work assured the pirates that nothing would be held back; everything they had would be handed over immediately.

"Fine," said the fisherman's son, "We expect nothing less. But where are your officers? Why aren't they here to greet us?"

The sailor looked dismayed, though the pirate leader wanted merely to congratulate the men who had bested him in sailing for the past half-year, and, if possible, to learn what sailing secrets they had used to do it.

"Below . . . tending to business . . . ." mumbled the frightened sailor, eyeing the planks below his feet as if he could see his absent superiors through them.

"Show me." But when the poor old sailor began to tremble, the pirate captain ordered his own men to search the ship. They soon found the officers in the crews' quarters, with the captain cowering in a storeroom behind some sacks of flour. A bit of stern questioning with a knife at his throat soon had him blubbering for mercy, and he led them to a little locked room off his own quarters. There the pirates, who already loathed this fat and cowardly captain, expected to find the profits he had hoarded from his crew and masters. What they found was more pathetic, and, as they learned, more valuable.

On the dirty floor, inside a cage barely large enough to hold him, lay curled a sickly boy, as thin as a skeleton, with half-closed eyes, and dry skin rubbed raw in places. He breathed in gulps, and a fine tremor passed at intervals over his whole body, as if he were shivering, though the air in the room was hot and foul-smelling. There was no sign of food or drink. A basin with a scoop near the cage held what appeared to be seawater with shreds of seaweed floating in it like sops.

The pirate asked the captain the meaning of this sight, whose pointless cruelty offended him. When the captain didn't answer right away, the pirate seized his hand and pressed his knife against the fat flesh of his palm. A line of blood welled out from the blade, and the captain squealed at the sight of it. Then he babbled his story.

The creature in the cage was no boy, but a water sprite they had captured. Sprites, as everyone knows, are masters of all aspects of waves and wind, and know the contrary currents that shift just under the surface, or the storm that is approaching on a cloudless day. The captain (he started to say "My officers," but when the pirate gestured with his knife admitted the decision had been his) thought that if he could force the sprite to be his navigator, he might gain advantage enough to stay ahead of both pirates and his competitors. Out of its element, the sprite weakened, but dashes of water revived it when they needed its advice.

The pirate jerked the point of his knife at the basin, unwilling even to say "Show me" to the merchant, whose throat he had to restrain himself from slitting on the spot.

The captain scooped up a bit of the fetid water and threw it over the caged sprite's legs. The sprite opened its eyes and drew in a wheezing breath. The sight revolted the fisherman's son. He ordered the sprite brought out of the cage and carried up to the upper deck, where it was laid carefully. Barrels were filled with fresh seawater, and long strands of seaweed were gathered. The seaweed was laid over the sprite, covering it like a wet green blanket. Seawater was ladled on it, from head to foot. The pirate captain and his two officers did this personally, while their men transferred the merchant ship's cargo to their own ship, making the merchant sailors do the heaviest and dirtiest work. They kept the fat captain and his officers sweating down in the bilge, and did not hestitate to use their fists to underscore their commands to such despicable seamen.

The sprite recovered slowly at first, then very rapidly. The cloudiness went out of its eyes, which became clear and sharp again; its breathing slowed and deepened; and its raw injured skin smoothed over and became subtly luminous, shining with a faint milky sheen as if soft light moved in its veins. It lay quietly collecting its strength, watching the men who tended to it;

then, without a prior movement, sprang to its feet with a swift fluid motion that was not in any way human, though something in human form performed it.

The pirates stepped back, startled at the sight despite all the wonders they had seen on the high seas. Within its dripping green strands, the sprite stood slim and straight, with a calm dignity in its upright posture that branded as even more despicable its wretched treatment at the hands of the merchants. Inclining its head toward each of the pirates in turn, and addressing the captain last, it spoke these words in its high clear voice, like a boy's except less reedy and more forceful:

You will find on Saturday
You on Friday next
You will dig till Neverday
And then you'll find what's best

WITHOUT ANOTHER WORD the sprite sprang to the gunwale and dove down into the water, so swiftly that in the second it took the amazed pirates to reach the side, they missed all but a white shimmer far below.

"Will you kill us now?" whimpered the merchant captain when the pirates had him and his officers brought before them. "I wouldn't dull my sword with you," said the fisherman's son. He locked the captain and his two officers in the cage in which they had kept the sprite, and threw the key overboard. Then he ordered his men to smash the instruments of navigation and tear up all the charts. "Learn to sail by the stars," he told the miserable seamen assembled before him, and handed the captain's hat and papers of command to a slow-witted cabin boy who had formerly emptied the captain's slops.

All that Saturday, the first pirate addressed by the sprite dug, from dawn to dusk, on as many beaches as he could reach. He found no treasure. That night, drinking under the stars, his two companions laughed at him, their jokes aimed also at themselves, since if one of them had been tricked by the sprite, all had. Still, every Saturday, the first pirate searched stubbornly, wherever he had a hunch treasure might be lurking, unable to believe that the graceful creature they had saved would stoop to deceiving him. Week after week, he found nothing.

Some months later, on a windswept coast where he was burying a particular friend, a fierce and foolish favourite who had died in a battle the day before, he struck a rock with his spade. The rock turned out to be no rock, but the metal ribbing on a wooden chest. When he opened it, the splendour of the wealth inside—jewels, coins of many countries, chains of gold and silver—sprang out to hurt his eyes with abundance, like a sun he was staring into. The tears he had shed for his friend started again. It was Saturday, he realized.

Within a year, the second pirate had found a treasure hoard even larger than this first, on a Friday as the sprite had foretold. The two were now in a position to retire and live like lords for the rest of their days. Loyally, however, they insisted on remaining with their friend, either to search for his reward together or to divide amongst them the treasure already found, just as they had always carved into equal shares the booty they plundered. But the fisherman's son would not accept their generosity, or deter them from enjoying their fortunes. He put them off at the next port, so they could arrange passage back to the village, where they planned to build great houses and live in the style of wealthy men. "I will join you as soon as I'm able, and we'll show the villagers how they underestimated us. Especially the women." The three friends laughed, and parted warmly, though in their heads rang the sprite's word that they feared to speak: *Neverday*.

LOOKING WITHOUT FINDING soon stops being a search and becomes a way of life, and that is what it became for the fisherman's son. At first, recalling his friends' heaped treasure chests, and the sprite's promise that he would find "what's best," he dug his spade eagerly into each new beach he came to. Finding nothing did not disappoint him, it only whetted his appetite more; after all, his friends had searched far longer than they expected, and had found their reward only when they had almost given up hoping for it. Sprites were curious creatures; *neverday* might only be their way of saying *a very long time*, or *a day when you least expect*. He continued his pirate ways, chasing down ships and plundering what they carried, celebrating each capture with feasts and drinking songs, even adding, though more slowly, to his savings chest—but, more and more, he lived mainly for those moments on a new beach, some patch of sand in a corner of the world, the sun just setting or just coming up . . . when, leaning on his spade handle to rest, he felt a peace he had never known before creep over him like a warm vine and send down roots deep into his heart.

He travelled to remote regions of the earth, wherever waves could carry him. Years passed. As a pirate who dug on distant beaches in the evening—or a digger on beaches who practiced piracy to reach them—he grew old. Too old, at least, to be chasing younger men for their coins, he thought. It was time to go home. But where was that? He was a vagabond of the waves. One day, he heard from a passing ship that his father, the fisherman, was very sick. His friends, the two rich pirates, had sent out word with every ship to try to reach him. At the next port, he bought passage on a fast schooner back to the village. What he had saved in his chest he divided among the men on his ship, according to the shares system they used. We'll keep it safe for your return, they said.

Spend it, he replied. I won't be coming back.

Arriving in the village a few days later, he found his mother and brother keeping a vigil around the body of his father, who had died the day before. The candlelight flickered over their few possessions, even more sparse and threadbare than he remembered. The hut was in disrepair, its roof leaking in places and leaning to one side owing to a crumbling of the foundation stones. His father, he learned, had been sick for more than a year, during which time he could fish only occasionally, and not at all near the end. His mother and his brother, the net-mender, had picked up what work they could, and had not been too proud to accept the bunches of

vegetables or occasional fish left on their doorstep. The three of them shared a dinner of soup and bread, trading stories of their years apart, happy to be reunited despite the sorrowful occasion.

The next day, the two brothers prepared to bury their father. Having no coffin, they wrapped him in his sail cloth. This was the only time the net-mender, who had kept his amiable nature despite infirmity and a hard life, threw a sharp glance at his brother. Have you really got nothing from those years? he asked him. The pirate shrugged. Get and lose, he said, is all I know. It's all there is . . . out there. He gestured at the sea beyond the docks.

And that—the sea—was where the brothers decided to bury their father instead of in the village graveyard. He had spent his days on the water. Their mother made no protest, though she would not go with them, saying her farewell to her husband with a kiss on his cold face before the net-mender sewed shut his shroud.

The pirate rowed them out from land, while his brother sat in the stern with their father's body. When they were out of sight of the village, he directed his brother to row along the shore, keeping close enough to land so that he could sight a beach he was looking for. The pirate did not question or argue. The one who stays has rights never to be disputed by the one who roams: that much he knew without being taught. Finally, a long way up the coast, his brother pointed to a certain small cove. There, he said.

When they had landed and brought their father ashore, the brothers stood awhile in silence beside the shrouded figure on the sand. Then the net-mender said, looking down at his father as if he could not easily lose the habit of their conversation, This was where he brought me once. It was after he first got sick, or when we realized how sick he was. He said that this was where he found himself, on the worst and best day of his life.

The net-mender, whose legs could support him only briefly now, sat by their father's body and watched while his brother dug the grave. His brother dug swiftly, with an almost savage energy, sweat falling from his brow, the muscles in his dark forearms jumping. When he struck something solid, it sent a shiver up his arms. What is it? called the net-mender.

But the pirate, grinning fiercely down into the hole, already knew. He saw it before he had uncovered even a corner of it. And he saw what would happen next. Once they had emptied the chest, the largest one yet, of its riches, they would lay the shrouded fisherman in it and return it to the ground. His father would receive a burial fit for him, and the three of them would live well for the rest of their days—

Or? Before he could raise the spade again, a competing vision invaded his mind. The sprites were devious. What if, this time, the chest itself were the treasure—a casket of solid gold, say, encrusted with gems? A fortune around an empty space. In that case, he resolved, he would still put his father into it and return it to the ground, surprising his simple brother with the finest gesture imaginable. A gesture entirely in keeping with the pirate's life, though no one might believe it who had not lived it with him. He stood beside the half-dug grave testing his resolve, and did not begin to dig again until he was sure he could do it. Now the net-mender was standing beside him, a puzzled look on his face. What is it, brother? he asked.

Without answering, the pirate set to work again. A few more spadefuls of damp sand uncovered a rusty metal corner and the cracked planking it had once protected. The top of the chest, though split and gaping in the middle, was the largest intact piece of the box. Below it the sides and bottom caved in to rot and splinters. Neither brother said anything, nor did they look at each other. The net-mender got down on his knees and helped his brother clear away the broken wood, setting aside the unbroken lid, which they laid over their shrouded father in the manner of a shield, then filled in the grave with sand, leaving it unmarked, and rowed back home in silence to the village.

ON A HILL across the bay from the fisherman's hut stand the two fine houses built by the pirates whom the sprites made rich. Both are married, with many children, whose playful cries echo through their rooms and gardens. The two men, not denying themselves any luxury, have grown stout with age, but they give generously to their friends and to the villagers that live below them, too. The villagers being as proud as they are poor, the former pirates must find ways to cloak their generosity: replacing the village dock because, they say, its rotting timbers might scrape their own fine pleasure boats; buying far more fish from a seller than they can use; hiring local tradesmen to build unneeded additions to their houses; and so on. But the poorest and proudest villager will take nothing from them, no matter how they disguise it. This is their former captain, the fisherman's second son. After his work day, he sometimes walks up the steep path to their homes, and sits with them on the terrace watching the sun set, eating their roasted meats and drinking their wine, telling the same stories and jokes they once told on the deck of the ship; all with undimmed gusto, as if the years and their divided fates were no more than bits of sea foam blown back from a wave;—but when he leaves, he leaves with nothing but the good memories they have shared. A proud man.

And a happy one, it seems; no longer restless, or at least not in the old sea-churning way. He has taken his father's place in the fishing boat, and, though not the fisherman his father was—and too old ever to learn so

much—his own knowledge of the sea and its creatures serves him decently, and with his still-strong body and stubborn will, he brings home enough to keep them fed. His brother, though mostly confined to the hut now, still mends nets, their own and others, and takes in other sewing work (the rich men send him what they can, under others' names). Working together, the brothers have repaired the sagging hut and reclaimed the neglected garden. Their mother no longer works; though gladdened to see her boys under one roof again, without her husband, she is aging rapidly.

Often, after a day of rowing and hauling nets, when supper is done, the former pirate takes his spade and walks to some part of the pebbly beach that stretches around the great bay. When he is out of sight of the village, he finds a place that is new to him, with some new angle on the sea and the orange fireball sinking into it. Pulling solitude around him like a cloak, he turns over sand and pebbles in a slow, meditative rhythm, accented with eager flurries when the spade strikes something hard.

He believes himself alone, but his friends live high enough to see him. They see everything in the village, and in coves and villages far beyond this one. Looking down from one terrace or the other, they watch the slowly digging figure, darkening as the night comes

on. The words they trade are the thoughts of an old conversation, which hardly varies except in the part taken by either man.

"A sad sight," one will begin. Let it be the richest pirate this time.

"Is it?" the second richest pirate will answer. And, after a pause, go on: "What was the best time of your life?"

"That's easy," says the richest pirate. "It was every Saturday before I found the treasure the sprites promised me."

"And for me it was Friday," says the second richest pirate. "That was when my blood raced. Waiting for treasure was the best. Not knowing when I would find it, and planning how I would spend it when I did."

"And?" says the richest pirate. And it is not impossible he will yawn, or stifle a yawn. This conversation is like the pipe and brandy that accompany it: something to be drawn out and savoured, warming the chest with a familiar tang.

"His whole life," the other will say, gesturing at the black bar bending and straightening far below, "has been those days of waiting and planning. He never sees a beach without thinking it could be the one. He never turns a spadeful of sand without thinking he is about to uncover emeralds, rubies, pearls, and gold."

Wear Me Last

Some months ago a young man got locked in a costume shop overnight. It happened purely by accident. The young man, who appears to be a student at the university, underfed and sullen-looking, fashionably unshaven, spent so long in the mask room at the back of the shop that the elderly proprietor, dozing over a book he had read before, forgot he was there. As there were no other customers, he put away his book, tidied up the cash area and left the shop, locking the front door behind him.

The video cameras that come on after hours recorded what happened next.

The student emerged from the back room and saw that he was alone in the shop. If he was surprised, he didn't show it. He smiled wryly, looked about, and returned to the display of masks.

Alone among the rows of crafted faces, he began posturing and pretending, trying on various masks and striking poses in them. At first a little shyly, with awkward hesitations, as if unable to believe he was unwatched; but then more exuberantly, as he gained confidence in his solitude and surrendered himself to the pleasures of pretending to be others.

He first selected a pirate mask. It had a red bandana, a black eye patch, a hooked nose, a purple scar down one cheek, and a bristling black moustache. Its rubbery texture suggested real, salt-weathered skin. Putting it on, he flourished an invisible sword, parried blows, and ran his enemy through.

An ape face was the next mask he tried. He smiled again, his mouth lifting at one corner, when he turned the mask around and saw *The Gorilla* printed on a white label. What else could it be? But the proprietor was a meticulous sort, perhaps to counteract what he saw as a carelessness in his usual customers: actors, students, "creative" types wanting to throw a memorable party. He treated them a bit stiffly, as if to ward off a frivolity encouraged by his line of work. Hallowe'en was the only season when he relaxed a little, and grew warmer and more convivial with them.

The student put on his King Kong face and beat his thin chest.

The Vampire worked better. The student was already dressed in black, and when Dracula's waxy face was in place, he unfastened all but the top button of his coat, making it more like a cloak, and then flung his arms out to the sides—*Haaah!*—while dropping his chin below his fangs.

He made his way slowly along the shelves on both sides of the narrow room. Always turning the mask around to read its label, even when the features made this unnecessary. Examining the life-like skin textures and detailed features and hairstyles, often bringing them close to his own face to do so. Every now and then trying another one on. *The Monk. The Alien. The Mummy. The Courtier. The Ghoul.*

At the end of the row, at the very back of the store, he came to a mask that was unlike any of the others. It was painted a dull white and had expressionless, rudimentary features: eye holes, a bulge for a nose, and a mouth slit. It looked like the model for a mask, or perhaps a mask that had been started and then abandoned. But why then was it on the shelf? The mask's label was not on the back, but scotch-taped to the forehead. *Wear Me Last*, it said. Scrawled in black marker on a torn square of paper, it did not seem like the work of the careful proprietor. Frowning in puzzlement, the student turned the mask around. No other label.

After staring for a few moments at the mask in his hands, he set it back on the shelf—delicately, as if he were handling a bomb or other dangerous device—and headed toward the front of the room. He seemed done with the masks. When he was almost out the door, however, he paused, looked thoughtful, and then, with a sudden frown, turned and strode back to the last mask. Without a pause, he put it on.

What happened next was strange to observe; especially in silence, though there was no overt indication that the young man made any sound.

At first, nothing happened. He looked about the room. He made no gestures (what gestures would he make with such a mask?). Then the mask began to glow. Considering what came next, this may have been due to a thinning of the mask's material, making it less opaque; in any case, it seemed to quiver with a faint white light. The young man stared at a spot high up in the room; it appeared that he could feel something taking place, but was not in pain or otherwise distressed by it. Gradually, the mask became translucent, the young man's features appearing blurrily, milkily, through it; and then, by degrees, ever more clearly, until he seemed to be wearing a mask of spotless glass, through which his features appeared with absolute clarity, even more clearly than they had appeared before, as if brought into sharper focus. But that was not the end. There was a further stage. The glass—or whatever rigid material it was—began visibly to soften and become mobile, settling around his features, dropping into the hollows below his cheekbones and molding exactly around his nostrils and jawline. Now the young man did show signs of distress: not pain, precisely, but alarm at what he sensed was occurring. His eyes widened and he plucked at the strap behind his head, but the strap, following the same progression as the front of the mask, had already disappeared into his hair. The process quickened now, and when he tore, too late, at the front of the mask, trying to find an edge he could lift off, his fingers left red welts on his own skin. The observers saw a final flicker, a dimpling of light, as the clear mask slipped below the level of his skin, like a glass plate slipping into a murky pond.

He looked quickly from side to side, as if expecting something to rush out at him. But he was evidently unharmed. He brought his hands up to look at them. He seemed as he had been—though shaken, certainly. He kneaded the skin of his face carefully, rubbing his forehead, nose, cheeks and jaw; his face clouding over, perhaps because they felt unchanged. He looked worried. When he turned and saw the empty shelf where the mask had been, he fled from the back room and from the store. The camera over the front door caught the tails of his long coat flying upwards as he ran down the street.

His departure tripped the door alarm, which brought the police, who summoned the yawning and dishevelled proprietor. The events caught by the camera were odd, certainly—one officer made a crack about "Higher learning" and his partner chuckled—but as there was no evidence of theft or any other crime, and nothing to do except to keep the film in case some student reported a mysterious illness or other aftereffect, the police left.

The proprietor, wide awake now, though he had yawned repeatedly to make the policemen leave, hurried into the back room. A new arrival came rarely, at intervals he couldn't predict, and the last time had been over a year ago. Eagerly, he began checking his inventory of masks. He never knew what, or where, it would be. He had wondered whether he might be better able to guess if he paid closer attention to his customers. But he had been in the business too long, and besides, that would ruin the surprise.

He found it wedged between *The Fighter* (cuts and bruises, a pulped nose and fat lip) and *The Diver* (goggles and regulator, wet plastered hair and bluish skin). It was a beauty. Literally. Luscious rosebud lips,

painted bright red; creamy cheeks, with an adorable little mole just above the corner of the upper lip, and a matching dimple on the other side; aquiline nose with excitingly flared nostrils; eyelids half-descended, and above them, dark black eyebrows, plucked and teased into naughty crescents; waves and ringlets of copious blonde hair, gloriously false.

The Starlet. The name came to him immediately, as it always did.

He wouldn't try her right away, not until he made the label.

He stood admiring the new arrival for a minute more, feeling his elation shade with a regret he had never been able to name. Was it that they came so rarely, or that they came so unexpectedly, with such inscrutable randomness, like the dropped valuable that gleams on a dark and deserted street? With no way to contact the owner, what can you do except give thanks for carelessness in your vicinity?

Perplexed and gratified, he went into the storeroom, where he reached into a carton to retrieve another blank.

...luscious dregs...

Sloth's Minions

*O*f all the thousands of gods and goddesses worshipped by humankind, Sloth alone had no helpers. What did he need them for? He had no sea to part, sun to drive, dead to judge, or message to deliver. He was Sloth. He lay around while eternities passed, doing the absolute minimum, never lifting a finger for anyone or anything.

Even so, from time to time, Sloth's vanity whispered to him that he, like any god, deserved a retinue. If the thought prodded him long enough, he would wander over to whatever council of gods was convening nearby and make his case. Lamely and halfheartedly, to be sure, with yawns he didn't hide, unwilling to break a sweat even on his own behalf.

The results were always the same. Whichever god was presiding would reply: "Tell us what you have undertaken that requires any assistance."

And Sloth, of course, had no answer, and couldn't be bothered inventing one. Dismissed amid laughter, he slumped away with a shrug and a belch.

Returning from one such flop, Sloth wondered if he wouldn't be better off recruiting his own minions from the legions of the lazy. They already followed him, after all, and only needed their service to be confirmed. Seeing three young men lounging outside a city's gates, he decided they would do.

These three slugs, all lazy to the core, sat on a patch of grass beside the road, their backs to a low wall, dozing or trading stories while a greasy cap did their begging for them. Hardly anyone threw in a coin, which didn't bother them in the least. They went on with their meandering anecdotes about the only subject they knew: their own inability to do an hour's work, and the riches they'd squandered by not being bothered to keep a grip on them. All of their stories, which amounted to lethargic boasts, sounded much the same. Family, friends, jobs, lovers—whatever bit of goodness life had drifted their way, they'd watched it slide off again, for simple lack of concern to keep it. Mostly they told the truth, since lying took a mental effort they wouldn't expend.

Listening for a bit from the crowded roadway, Sloth decided they would serve well enough. He dropped a ten dollar bill in the cap to catch their attention, then briefly laid out who he was and what he proposed.

"You don't look like what you say," interrupted one of the wastrels suspiciously. He, like his two companions, was dressed for comfort in baggy clothes, rubbed shiny around the hips; had a thin but flabby-looking body; and a weak, shifting face you wouldn't trust to do the smallest errand. Sloth was clean-shaven, with a neat haircut, and wore smart, new-looking clothes. He looked capable enough. "Yeah," said another of the beggars, "You look like you're doing fine."

"I can't be bothered to look otherwise," said Sloth. "I wear whatever most people are wearing, and talk a good game. That gets me by with the least trouble."

The three appeared to take this in. "And we'll be with you for good?" asked the beggar who hadn't spoken yet, returning to Sloth's proposal.

"For all time," answered Sloth.

"Doing nothing."

"That's all."

"But we'll be dead," said the first beggar.

"Immortal," said Sloth. "Excused from life. And, after all," Sloth went on, seeing the wastrels hesitate over this point, "what has life done for you lately?"

This seemed to settle them. They would become Sloth's minions. Except—during this little parley Sloth had remembered that he didn't have the power to make anyone his minion. It was only a passing daydream. He didn't have any powers, since he'd never needed any. Furthermore, he'd already spent more time and effort than he cared to on this conversation; he was ready to move on. As a parting gesture, he'd have a little fun with these three, as long as it took no effort.

He proposed a challenge. They would demonstrate their worthiness to be his minions by coming up with a way to find fame and fortune without lifting a finger. Doing as little as possible, each beggar would have to acquire a name for himself or make a lot of money. Whoever found the easiest way would be Minion Number One, with all due honours and privileges. Sloth could not stay to watch the contest, but he would leave his clerk to record and pass on the results.

"Who's that?"

Sloth pointed to a large boulder on the other side of the road.

"A rock?" said all three at once.

"Do you know anything that gets by with less strain?" Sloth asked. The three looked at one another, then back at Sloth, who said, "Believe me, he'll get the

job done. And without any fuss to show how hard he's working."

With that, Sloth stepped back among the citizens moving to and fro along the road; the beggars squinted to find him, but he blended away from sight; it was like following a leaf in a forest. They began casting about for ways to satisfy Sloth's terms. One would suggest a do-nothing scheme, then another would point out the flaw in it—the unavoidable bit of effort it might entail—and suggest a better one. Ideas came to them quickly, and it soon became the most animated conversation they'd ever had. What Sloth proposed, they realized, was trickier than they'd thought. Getting something for little was no great challenge, they'd spent their lives doing it; but bringing that little down to nothing, or close to it—that was tough. Which was only reasonable, they agreed, considering that an eternity of indolence was the prize.

They dreamed up sure-fire schemes, and shot them down. Whenever one hit on a promising scam, he addressed himself to the rock sitting opposite, like a lawyer pleading his eloquence before a particularly stern and impassive judge. The rock, of course, betrayed no reaction; though it was possible, by the play of sun and shadow on its surface, to imagine all kinds of thoughts and emotions passing through it. Finally, one beggar declared that he had it. He sat up and, with a smile at the rock, told his companions of his plan.

The trick, he said, was so obvious that they should have thought of it sooner. It was hiding in plain sight. They'd been looking for ways to make a name without effort, but why not let somebody else make the name. This was his brainstorm: find a person who has already won fame and fortune, murder him or her, and their name will never be mentioned again without yours attached to it. Like a flea riding on an elephant: you go everywhere the great creature does, without ever moving your legs. And what's more, if you pick the right place to do it, you'll be executed for your crime, which will spare you the often long and, let's face it, arduous business of leaving this life. For the price of squeezing a trigger, you'll arrive at Sloth's door with a name to rank with anyone's. All ready to become Minion Number One.

The other two nodded slowly, unable to find fault with his logic, though the mention of death perturbed them a little. It was a detail that tended to get lost in their discussions. But they found no flaw in the scheme itself, and envied its simplicity.

"Well, good luck finding your own!" said the beggar with the scheme, getting to his feet. With a grin at the rock, he strode off importantly into the crowds heading toward the city, showing more energy in his step than his friends had ever seen.

A few days later, having concluded that the scheme was just hot air after all, hollow boasting of the kind they were all expert at, they were astonished to wake up from a doze at the sound of their companion's name coming at them from every direction. People were yelling it, hissing it, asking it, whispering it; some were even blubbering it with tears streaming down their faces. People going to the city, and people coming from it. Suddenly, his name was common as a curse. What's up? they asked a passerby, who was shocked that they hadn't heard. At a concert, their former companion had shot a beautiful and beloved young singer, her name familiar even to the indolent beggars. Her outraged fans had beaten him to death on the spot.

The two beggars absorbed this news in stunned silence. He had done it, after all. Though being beaten to death by a multitude didn't sound quite like the clean and painless exit he had imagined.

"Still," one said, "for sheer sloth, his achievement will be hard to top."

Some days later, the two were awakened from an afternoon nap by the chink of coins dropping into their begging cap. They looked up to see a smartly-dressed young woman looking down at them. She carried a notepad and pen.

"Excuse me," she said. "But I'm a reporter investigating—" And she mentioned the murdered celebrity and his killer, their former begging companion. Doing her research, she'd met a man from a flophouse who claimed to have known the killer. He told her a fantastic story of the god Sloth and the deal he'd offered to find suitable minions; over a bottle of cheap wine, the killer had babbled it to him. Other reporters had dismissed it as a lunatic's drivel. But she smelled a story that, true or not, might be worth something, and had followed the lead of—she checked what was written in her notebook—"two worthless fools killing time outside the city gates."

"Would that be you?" she asked hesitantly.

The two nodded eagerly, too indolent even to take offence. They'd been feeling slighted that in all the furor their names had never come up. Quickly, the reporter got down to business. Her magazine was prepared to pay good money for exclusive rights to the story. All they had to do was give her a detailed interview and let her take a couple of pictures. She named the figure they'd earn. The two gaped at each other, unable to hide their shock that, without their moving a muscle, money and fame were coming to find them. At the same time, staring at each other, a devious look came into their eyes. One of them beat the other to the punch.

"I can give you everything you need. There's no need to involve him at all," he said, jerking his thumb at the other, who made no protest. "But I'll take twice what you're offering. And rather than interview me, you write down the story just as you heard it, and if it looks okay, I'll sign my name."

The reporter wrinkled her nose in distaste, but agreed to his terms, saying she'd be back soon. The story-selling beggar sat back, pleased with himself, sure that for receiving money and fame for a signature, he'd not only outdone his predecessor, but set the bar too low for anyone else to crawl under. He directed a look of satisfaction at his companion, who seemed unconcerned, and then a broad smile at the rock, Sloth's clerk, who looked back just as impassively.

When the reporter returned, the story-seller looked over her pages and saw that she had what she needed. Minus a few unimportant details, she'd dug up the whole chain of outlandish events, from Sloth's appearance to their friend's eager departure for the city. He double-checked the spelling of his own name. Then scrawled his signature at the bottom. The lawyer handed him a cheque and snapped his picture.

"Now that we're done," she said, taking a careful step back toward the road, "I don't mind saying that your way of life sickens me. I feel dirty just dealing with you." She turned to the third beggar, who still hadn't said a thing. "How does it feel," she smirked, "to come last in a race of losers? Don't you even have one detail to add to my story?"

"Just this," he said. "Be sure to mention who won the prize without even signing his name."

And, rising with more alacrity than he'd shown in years, he walked straight into the path of an oncoming truck, beaming at the rock right up to the moment of impact.

The bested beggar gaped, then scowled, as the reporter hurried away from the scene.

The next time Sloth importuned the other gods for helpers, he told this story, which had made the rounds and got back to him eventually. The other gods roared with laughter at the hapless beggars and at Sloth's presumption in trying to justify himself by so sorry an undertaking. The god presiding that day said:

"You're deluded if you think it's any challenge to get men to throw away their lives. Still, you've given us some entertainment, which is more than we've had from you before. Let us consider your needs, and provide you with the assistance you deserve."

Shrugging, Sloth shambled off. After some detours he returned home to find his clerk, the rock, waiting for him. Circling it, he saw that it offered him a seat, a backrest, and a patch of shade for sleeping—amenities he's been taking advantage of ever since.

The Glass Garden

"Unlucky the child with old, sick parents," runs the saying, "for she grows up too soon." But curses usually work as well in reverse, and Penelope was unlucky in just the opposite way: her parents were so perennially young and strong, happy as a pair of newlyweds and without a wrinkle or care between them, that there seemed no need for their daughter to grow up at all. And yet, surrounded by games and laughter, with parents more fun than she could ever hope to be, Penelope did develop serious ways early on. While her parents frolicked like a couple of kids, she was sober and unsmiling (which her parents and their friends loved to tease her for, saying she could steal men's hearts for the price of a dimple), a fine-boned girl with dark eyes to match her hair, who was happiest when tucked up in some corner of the house by herself, reading book after book.

"Come and see our scholar at work," her parents would cry at the parties they loved to give, and flinging open the door to the room Penelope was in, would announce to the friends behind them, "There she is, burning the midnight oil!" And the friends would laugh good-naturedly and pat her on the head, saying, "Don't wear out your eyes. Or your brain!" And Penelope would smile back, partly because she was mannerly and polite, but also because she knew they meant no harm and merely loved a good time, unable to understand the things that gave her pleasure. And therein lay a kind of safety, too. She loved her charming, heedless parents, but she learned early on to keep a prudent distance from them. They loved beautiful things, but they were hard on them. And she had no wish to be swept to the floor and smashed, like the wine glasses and porcelain plates that kept getting batted off tables by people telling boisterous jokes. A bit like a spy in her own house, she picked her way carefully from day to day, observing her parents at play and figuring out what they wanted and when, and keeping to herself her own wishes and intentions.

If this makes her sound cold or unhappy, that is wrong. For dreams and desires hopped like rabbits in her head; it was only that she knew she was in a place where very few of these warm, small creatures should venture out into the open.

Her parents kept a large, flourishing garden behind their house; and though they were wealthy enough to employ a gardener (and did not need to work at anything unless they chose), they loved to be outdoors and active in the sun. And that is where their pale, bookish daughter often came upon them: two sun-dark, shapely people, her mother reaching to pick a pear while her father planted a kiss on her outstretched golden throat; or her father crouching to weed between the vegetables, while her mother ran her hand through his thick brown curls. "Oops, a little ghost just spied us," one or the other would say, emerging from their stolen moment to catch sight of their daughter. "Better not give her any ideas," her father would grin, looking a trifle embarrassed at being caught. "She doesn't have those kinds of ideas," her mother would say, a little more tartly, narrowing her eyes at the intruder. But before the moment could lengthen too uncomfortably, the lovers would resume poking and teasing each other, their eyes twinkling with private jokes, and their daughter, thankful to be forgotten, would be hurrying away on her own errand.

Usually she was on her way to her glass garden.

THE GLASS GARDEN was hers because nobody else wanted it. It was laid out in a corner of the property that no one but Penelope ever visited, a neglected place though a protected one, first by the paving stones surrounding the oval bed, then by a low wrought-iron fence, about two feet high, around the perimeter, which together ensured that no one could blunder accidentally among the delicate stems and petals. Someone had taken the trouble to shield the garden, though who that might be neither of her parents could say. History was not something that interested either of them, for obvious reasons. They were having too much fun to think of the world as anything but a carnival that had popped into existence yesterday, with them as its first two giggling visitors.

She listened for a moment, to make sure the voices laughing and calling were still distant, before she stepped over the fence and knelt at the edge of the glass garden. It was a wonder. Clear glass stems suffused with greenish light; tall tulips in orange-and-pink, brilliant yellow, red—luscious cups whose dregs were smoky brown stamens tipped with beads of honey pollen; velvety roses, pink and red and white; purple and blue hyacinth clusters; tall blades of iris, orange puffs of marigold; glass flowers of all kinds, even, down near the ground, for variety, the little green and purple mounds of hen and chickens—and all shot through with the sunlight caught by the facets of glass and sent

shooting and bouncing in a hundred different directions, with a dozen moods and characters: softly pulsing and throbbing on cloudy days, fiercely glinting on bright; hurting the eyes with glitter when the snow lay round about and multiplied and intensified the reflections. Even the bed's porcelain base had been done in a deep earthy brown, which showed through between the witty litter of straw and wood chips worked this way and that, as if strewn, above it.

With all of its maker's art of patient and loving attention glancing from every detail, the glass garden was Penelope's natural home. She felt connected through it to the slow, steady pulse of art—and, through that, to the pulse of the unseen artist, with whom she was more than a little in love. Years had passed, inside her parents' endless sunny day; and though her parents took no notice, or noticed but then forgot, she had left childhood behind. Not only was she capable of romantic ideas, as her mother's narrowed eyes accused, but these consumed her thoughts. But, as always, her dreams differed from those of her parents. If theirs belonged to the knight and princess phase of romance—stolen glances and kisses behind a screen of grape leaves—then hers already looked beyond this to something older and quieter; and outside the castle walls, too, beyond king and queen to a vision of two scholars reading by the fireside, looking up from their books to share a moment, a memory. The stolen glance and kiss were still there, but more refined, more (in her view) rounded and intoxicating, as the cup of finished wine is to the grape buds it started from.

Dreaming such thoughts, she stared into the restlessly flickering fire of the glass garden. Cautious almost to a fault, she seldom reached out to touch it, and when she did so, she would only let a trembling finger graze a flat and sturdy-looking surface—a veined green leaf, say, at the base of a stalk—whose smooth coolness still surprised, though not as much as when summer sun made it hot, like the rim of a dish left too near an oven.

ONE DAY AFTER a rain, when she was tending her garden, as she put it, she heard a small, bright sound in the damp air. She listened. When it came again, she recognized the trill of a cricket, calling from somewhere nearby. Peering into the grass beyond the wrought-iron fence, she cocked her head when it chirped again, but as usual, the tiny voice seemed to hop about, coming from here, then here, and she could not locate the source. Silence. And she waited. The next chirp seemed to come from right beside the fence, from the slick grass blades almost touching it. She stared at the spot without blinking, waiting to see the grass stems twitch when it crawled, which was about the only way the little black ventriloquist would betray its position. What if it springs right into the glass garden!? she thought, picturing the black and hard-shelled—but living—body moving its long legs among the rigid glass stems. It gave her a queasy thrill to imagine it, and she realized she had never seen a living creature among the glass blooms: not a ladybug, not a wayward toad, not even a butterfly or cabbage moth flitting above them. Even such small creatures know where their living lies, she thought, a little sadly.

The cricket trilled loudly, clear and close. With a start, she realized it was already in the garden. There! behind the rose stems!—the sound sprang out again, sharp as glass within the glass; and without thinking she plunged her hand in after it, hungry to trap or rescue it; perhaps even to crush it—in her eagerness she couldn't say.

Her thumb caught one of the rose stems as she slipped her hand between them. It broke with a clean snap, and fell into splinters on the porcelain bed. Oh! She darted a look behind her, her heart catching when she realized she couldn't hear her parents, who were seldom quiet; but she couldn't see them either, and she turned back to the damaged garden, hearing her own heart thudding in her chest. There she saw the cricket that had started it all, making its way along the cedar chip illusion. Except—

Leaning in to get a better look, she saw that it was no illusion. A real black cricket made its way slowly—even a bit ponderously, like an old man with a pack on his back, she thought smiling—along a trail of wood chips and straw that were just as real as it was. She could almost smell—or she could smell! very faintly—the spice of the damp wood chips, the must of the straw bits; and, leaning even closer in, she saw the cricket's feet slip and scramble on the chips and then sink into the crumbled earth between them. Beside this little scene, and ahead of it, were the coloured porcelain and stems of the glass garden's base, and where the two scenes met was a thin wavery blur, a film of humid air not quite in focus. As she watched, entranced, this film, and the harder edges around it, pressed in upon the cricket-walk-scene from all sides, making it shrink and then suddenly wink from view, as if a door had closed slowly but firmly, and then swiftly, with a click. Like a figure in one of her books who has witnessed something uncanny, she rubbed her eyes and stared, and rubbed her eyes and stared—but nothing changed anymore in front of her. The glass garden was as it had always been.

That night she had a dream. The dream seemed like a continuation of what had happened in the glass garden. Both times she felt as if a door had opened suddenly and she was standing on the threshold peering through at what went on beyond it. Her eyes felt rinsed by the newness of what she saw. She peered eagerly, and a bit anxiously, stuffing her eyes with details, knowing that the door would swing shut just as suddenly—she felt it poised on its hinges. Ahead of her stood a man in a study or library; an older man, dignified and well-dressed, he stood with his back to her, looking out a small window. Penelope couldn't see what was beyond the window, but the light that came through it, flowing around him, together with the bookshelves reaching to the ceiling on either side of the window, made him seem to be standing in a stained glass window, or an illuminated page in a book, whose title might be *Knowledge*. Or, thought Penelope in her dream, *Freedom*. The brightness of the light coming from outside made the room seem shadowy, though it was daytime, and the shadow thickened back from the window to where she stood watching, in a kind of night. The scene seemed silent at first, so silent she might have heard a clock ticking; but then she was aware of a low droning music, a kind of chanting, or rumbling, that she then—these changes happened at abrupt, but regular, intervals, as if she were climbing step by step into another world—understood was the man speaking, in a calm low voice, but in a language she didn't know. *I'm dreaming*, she thought, and then, *I wonder if he'll turn*. The possibility set up a gnawing in her stomach, and she thought firmly, *Time to wake up. Open your eyes.*

But her eyes were already open, she realized. She was staring at her own bedroom, with its smaller shelves of books, and its dolls and figurines, gifts of holidays past. These things still partook of the scene in the library, one dark replacing the other only slowly, the man staring out his window where her dolls stared back at her. The transposition only sped up at the end, hastening to that click. Just as the glass garden had reclaimed the space occupied briefly by the cricket. Slowly swinging . . . shutting . . . shut.

Was I dreaming? she thought. Where was I? Where am I? And her thoughts swam confusingly, though she did not feel tired in the least.

The next morning, while her parents picked strawberries in adjacent rows—bobbing up every so often with a cry to tuck an especially plump one into the other's mouth, or—"Unh unh"—to tease and pop it into one's own—Penelope stepped over the iron fence and went round to the other side of the glass garden from where she'd knelt the day before. There was no back or front to the garden, since the rows were arranged to face out all ways and the paving stones allowed an approach from every side, but on this side she was near the hedge that marked the edge of their property, close to a shed where the former owners had probably kept tools. Standing here gave her a view back through the gardens to her house—a safer view, she'd always known, letting her see anyone coming, but also distracting her from the glass garden itself. Today, though, was not a day to get lost in daydreams. Today she needed to keep her house in view.

And she needed to stand, not kneel. Looking down, she spotted two glass flowers she could just reach, close to the centre, standing a little lower than their neighbours. She reached down and snapped one off near the base. With a flick of her wrist she knocked it to the porcelain, where it broke with a powdery pop into slivers and dust. Then its neighbour; she did the same to it. Still standing, but bending low to see, she peered down the stretch of road that had opened to her view. It was a country lane, with trees clustered close on either side, the sunlight through their moving leaves making dappled patterns on the packed brown dirt. Up the way a bit, she saw the trees thin to bushes,

lilacs perhaps, and then open out onto what looked like the soft greens and browns of a field—

The view closed. Not swiftly, but decidedly, as it had the day before. First the creeping fog edge, nibbling it back, then the quick swallow, like a gulp.

That night, when the other door opened in her sleep (or at least, when she had her eyes tightly closed, to make it happen faster), she saw a stillness, a hint of tension in the shoulders and neck of the man beside the window, as if he sensed her behind him and was about to turn. She was afraid, and not afraid. The dark browns and golds in his hair were a blend of the wood chips, the straw, and the packed earth of the road. Would his eyes be green?

When she returned to the glass garden the next afternoon, her heart sank to see that the hole made by the two snapped flowers was more obvious than she'd thought. The artist had done his work too well, grouping the blooms with a casualness that mimicked natural profusion but which had a symmetry easily disturbed. Even the first hole, from the broken rose, seemed to glare out at her like an eye. She saw that she would not be able to proceed as she had planned, granting herself gradually larger views of the world behind—behind or within—the glass garden. Standing a few moments above it, she felt disconsolate . . . and

then determined. Going round to where she'd been yesterday, she knelt down and, rather brutally, snapped off three daisies standing right at the edge, rapping with the backs of her fingers low down on their stems—pop, pop, pop.

Beyond the fields, which were covered with a variety of low grasses and clover, as if they might have been farmed but not recently, stood a small, neat house, more like a cottage than a farmhouse, though rather dark, at least on this side, where only a single arched window broke the stone-and-timber wall.

"We're going to spend the day tomorrow with the—," said her mother that night at dinner, naming the childless couple down the lane whom they counted as their closest friends. "We won't be back till late. Will you be all right on your own?"

She nodded, and her father said, "She's not a child, remember. She's growing up on us."

And her parents beamed at her, not with sidelong glances and a quick return to their own conversation, but straight on, for long moments that stretched tenderly; as if their eyes were portholes usually fogged by the heat of the ship, which had cleared suddenly, and Penelope, not knowing what had wiped or cooled them, didn't know either whether to feel grateful or sad, as she felt both, in a complex welling, as the clear round panes showed both the greenish sea, close and sloshing, and the departing shore's toy-like spires and roofs, receding.

THE ROAD she was walking on was packed firm; the spring and early summer had been dry. How different it felt to be walking somewhere when you knew you would not be retracing your steps. Her eyes drank everything in, and she kept looking from side to side, afraid to miss a single detail. The air had a sharp, singed smell, with hints of coming rain, advance cool puffs of it. The smells of the new place had come to her a second before its sights, when the crash and splintering of the smashed glass garden were still echoing in her mind, waves of tinkling breakage, and she had let fall the rake she had swung with such abandon and, with eyes pressed shut, drawn in a great, slow breath to steady herself before she looked.

Out in the field, past the green bushy lilacs, the walking was still easy. The land was lumpily humped and furrowed, like plasticine kneaded and tugged— she wondered again what it had been used for. Whatever its uses, they were long past. A lush carpet of low grasses and clover, dotted with wildflowers, felt spongy and soft as carpet underfoot. But the carpet was bunched, with those sudden lumps and knolls, and she stepped carefully to avoid twisting her ankle. Easy as it was, the walking tired her.

Clouds built quickly overhead, and before she was halfway to the house, she felt the first drops of rain. Cool spatterings on her face, and then more stillness, a fresh waiting, while the piled clouds darkened and rumbled. The hail began when she was almost at the house, which was probably just as well, because she had been wondering if she would be brave enough to knock on the door when she got there. Now, with the hard lumps pelting her, she just hurried forward with her arms flung over her head, ducked in under the peak of roof, and turned the knob.

Inside, in a narrow vestibule, she stood for a moment getting her bearings. There was a dull beating in her head, and she was very tired. The clattering on the roof trailed off and stopped. Sun slanted through a window, the way it will sometimes an instant after the end of a summer storm. But there was no window, as she saw a moment later. Only a flickering, irregular kind of light, making a part of the room glow softly, then fall dim again, then brighten—as if lamps placed here and there couldn't decide whether to stay on or off. Except that she didn't see any lamps.

Someone else was in the house. She could feel him . . . and feel that it was *him*. Slowly and unsteadily

—what has happened to my legs? she wondered—she crossed to the doorway and stepped through it into a larger room. The intermittent beams of light played over furniture and surfaces. The bookcases of her dream were there, two of them, but merely standing against the far wall, not framing the arched window. Though there was a window; yes, arched; and filled with a gray light. No one at it.

She turned at a sound, and saw an old man smiling kindly at her from in front of a stove. The sudden sight of him startled her, but did not frighten. Nothing familiar was in his face, but nothing fearful either. He was old and stooped, with wisps of white hair dressing his baldness. He was clothed with old-fashioned formality: a dark gray cardigan over his black trousers and white shirt, and a dark, perhaps navy bowtie with light dots on it. He had a wooden spoon in one hand, and he turned with it to a small pot he was stirring on the stove.

"I saw you coming back," he said with his back to her. "Yesterday a bit. And then this morning."

Back was what she thought he said. He was saying more now, but it had become the garbled rumbling of her dream, the drone that might be music or another language. It rumbled comfortably, like thunder in a bottle, and then, just as she was beginning to ignore it,

turned into normal speech she could understand. "We'll drink this outside in the garden when it's ready," he said now, clear as a bell. And then began rumbling again, fussing in the light that glowed and dimmed, illuminating him and then leaving him in shadow, as he took a jar from a shelf and added a pinch to whatever he was cooking.

Constant inconstancy was the law here. Or inconstant constancy. It worked either way, she saw.

Now she was sitting at a wooden table, with no memory of having crossed to it. Though it was just in time: her legs felt like stumps beneath her. Looking from the funny old man to the window, she remembered why she'd come. Questions popped into her mind, like bubbles in a froth of sudden comedy. *Where's your son? Or grandson? Which is better?* she thought, and brought her hand up to stifle a giggle. A cramped old claw with great knuckles hung in front of her, attached to a withered arm draped with loose, brown-spotted skin. It looked odd, distinctly and abruptly odd, but not surprising or out of place. Or no more so than anything else in this funny little house. Everything here could startle, nothing surprise.

A light went off. And then came on again. Brighter, now. They were outside at a little round table on a kind of patio. The air was cooler after the

rain. It smelled fresh. She closed her eyes. She opened them. Had he helped her—carried her?—outside, to this chair? Was that the effort that had made his face go red?

Strange, she thought. I was a girl this morning . . . and now this. And yet I don't feel any different than I ever did.

". . . Drink it slowly," he was saying. "Don't rush."

And looking down she saw a cup in her hands—How did *that* get there? she thought—and set it down on the saucer with a clatter.

He was rumbling again, his lips moving around a garble, his small old hands curled around his own cup. Beyond him, colours in a handful caught her eye. She leaned to the side and raised her head to see them. Inside a square of short grass bordered by a low, trimmed hedge, the flowers in an oval bed lay twisted every which way, some knocked flat and broken, some struggling to rise, a few spared and erect.

"Yes," he said, nodding, following her gaze. "It was the hail that did it. All in a few angry seconds. They'll come back, though, most of them. No worries."

Something in the way he said this, nodding over the cup in his hands, as if addressing it instead of her, filled her with a strange cold fright; and at the same time ordered her to look behind herself. When she did, her parents were leering at her from two feet away, their faces huge and self-delighted. They had followed her! Even here! She gasped, and would have dropped the cup had she still been holding it. She covered her eyes against their grinning, and felt herself shaking, trembling like a leaf all over. Through her clamped fingers, she felt a wet warmth sliding, and realized she was crying. Crying as she hadn't let them make her cry in years. What was happening to her here?

"Pet, pet," he was saying. Or perhaps it was "Pen, Pen . . . ." He pried at her hands, his fingers weak against her fear; and then she let him lift them away. His strange face was kind; it meant no harm. And when he began talking again, his words were clear and free of the rumbling; though what they said made only a cloudy kind of sense, they distracted her from the frights at her back; in a way she didn't understand, they kept them from reaching her. "It's only our stone pair. Our laughing lovers," he said, affecting a chuckle to comfort her. "Look around at them, you'll see." She wouldn't, not in this light. So bright it was, glaring, just when she wouldn't have minded some of the flickering and dim.

She looked down at the thin old hand patting her own on the table top. She had a fleeting sense of having

reached a safe place, even if she'd missed the man in the arched window.

"It was my fault. My mistake," he was murmuring, to her but with his head lowered, as if in apology. As if she could—forgive him? "It was the right charm, I thought. A charm to make the living lifeless, and the lifeless living. It would keep you safe. Keep you near."

He looked up guiltily, his eyes pink-rimmed. "I've got it now," he said. "It went too far, before. Or not far enough. But I've got it now," he said again.

He waited, as if expecting her to say something, and then, with a sigh, looked around the garden and got to his feet. Gathering the cups and saucers, he said, "Come inside, now. Come inside."

A LIGHT OFF, then on. Then almost off. Left low.

The old man was asleep beside her. That did not seem strange. Her body ached and she was glad at last to be lying down. Something warm moved in her chest. It shifted, and seemed to slide a layer further down inside her. She heard her heavy-footed parents moving upstairs, then all around her, thumping and clumping in their lifelong gleeful chase. Quickly, while there was still time, she stole outside and found the two glass figurines where she had hidden them in the shed. She stepped back over the iron fence and placed them carefully amid the slivers and shards of glass: the little bent gardener with his hoe, and his equally ancient wife with her bonnet and rake. No more than four inches high, they were her delicate rebuke to the huge and rigid figures locked in their embrace over by the trellis hung with sweetpeas. She wanted to see their faces when they found them, but didn't dare let them catch her. Any second now, the echo of what she had done would reach their slow ears and they would lumber over here, and discover—

But she would be safe inside, in the best hiding place she'd found yet, clutching a treasured old book as she listened for the distant grunts of surprise. And then, before the stamp and crunch of boots, the echo of faroff tinkling—in the pause of life simply astonished at itself—

Through that pause, a door she had left ajar, she would slip and be gone.

Falling Water

Lars and Elskelyn had been dancing partners for many years, but lately they had fallen out of step. They could still find the rhythm at the heart of a song, but each heard that rhythm at a different speed. Lars began to move a step or two faster, sometimes so much faster that Elskelyn cried, "Slow down, slow down. I can't keep up." Whereas Elskelyn, it seemed to Lars, always lagged at least a half measure behind, swaying in such a dreamy manner that he snapped, "Pick up the pace! We've lost the beat!"

Dancing, which had been their most effortless joy together, became a tense and clumsy stumble, and they soon found excuses to avoid it. If either of them wanted to try a new pattern of steps, it was easier to do it alone, when the other was away. Though they still slept and ate under the same roof, they seemed to live in different zones, moving to clocks that could no longer be synchronized.

Despondent over this, for they loved each other deeply, they walked out of town to find an old woman who, it was said, sold charms to treat strange maladies. They found the forest track their neighbours told them of, and had gone a good distance down it (they even walked at different paces now, so that Lars had to keep stopping and waiting, trying not to look impatient, for Elskelyn to catch up)—when they came upon a chubby little boy tending a low fire.

"Hello," Lars called, reaching him first. But the boy, who had scruffy red hair and a freckled face, smudged with dirt in places, merely shot them a sullen glance and continued his work by the fire. They watched him. Despite his lumpish body, he had quick, clever hands with which, using a small sharp knife, he fashioned objects out of wood and bark. These were laid in a row on a flat rock, like wares set out for sale, even though no other customers were in sight, and he showed no interest in Lars and Elskelyn.

While they watched, he removed two slender sticks he had been charring in the embers and placed them to one side to cool. He took another lying there and, with deft flicks of his blade, sharpened its blackened tip. On a square of birchbark, he used the charcoal stick to sketch a forest scene: two trees, a pool, and a bubbling waterfall. After a few seconds, the simple black lines began to glow with colour. Greens and blues, and the browns and grays of rocks appeared—until the fast sketch resembled a painting done in rich oils, almost a little window into an actual forest.

Lars and Elskelyn exchanged a look of wonder, but when the boy passed the drawing stick behind him, shoving it toward them as if he hoped they would take it and move on, Elskelyn said quietly, "It's lovely, but we're dancers."

The boy half-turned and scowled. He seemed bad-tempered, or displeased in particular by what she had said. When he resumed fussing over his fire, the couple felt they'd been dismissed, but they stayed to watch out of curiosity. From a little pot of water standing in the ashes to one side, he retrieved two strips of what looked like green willow wood. Though tiny bubbles in the pot told that the water was near boiling, his hand went in and out without starting. With fast movements that Lars and Elskelyn had trouble following, he cut the willow strips to size, bent them into rings, and fitted each with a clasp of a different, darker wood. He shoved them behind him with the same rude gesture.

As soon as they put on the willow bracelets, which fit their wrists exactly, Lars and Elskelyn felt the urge to dance. Unembarrassed by the boy's presence, they held each other and began moving slowly to a tune that entered their heads at the same time. They smiled with shy pleasure that after such a long interruption their steps again meshed perfectly. Somehow, by some magic in the willow rings, Lars heard the tune a little slower, and Elskelyn a little faster, and they glided through a few figures as one person.

Suddenly remembering the boy, they stopped, and Lars said, "We should pay—"

But the boy was gone. Though they could not have been dancing more than half a minute, there was no sign of his pot or sticks or finished wares, and dirt was kicked over the embers, which steamed through it like angry breaths.

Despite this unfortunate ending, the meeting with the boy began the happiest period in the dancing couple's life. Wearing the willow bracelets, they danced better than ever before. So well, in fact, that their dancing gave pleasure not only to themselves and to their neighbours who cleared a space at gatherings to cheer and clap them on, but even to strangers in sometimes distant towns, who invited them to dance in public in return for lodging and a small sum. Thus, in middle age, they finally found themselves able to earn a modest living doing what they loved.

It was a pleasant dream that continued for several years, before troubles reappeared to warn of an awakening.

They began to go out of step again. Not often, at first, and not by much—but then, they were expert dancers, who noticed the slightest wobble in the patterns they traced together. They quarreled for the first time in years, each blaming the other when their timing went off. Then, ashamed of their harsh words, they thought to blame the willow bracelets. No good lasted forever. For years, by some magic of their maker, the willow rings had remained soft and supple as fresh wood; lately, however, they had begun to dry and show fine cracks, as if age was finally turning them brittle.

"Let's take them off. They don't owe us anything," Lars said, and pinched the slim band of wood encircling his wrist, as if to snap it off. But Elskelyn reached out and stopped him. "No," she said firmly.

For there was something else—a new kind of error in their dancing—which she had noticed before Lars, and which made her fear the willow bracelet, as a thing she could not correct because she did not understand it well enough. For the first time in their lives, she was jumping ahead of Lars. She was hearing the music ahead of him and hurrying to match it, while he was hearing a slower tempo and lagging behind. It wasn't obvious, because they were used to a different kind of misstep, but when Elskelyn explained, and they tried an old and simple figure, Lars saw that she was right.

They agreed to take the forest track and find the boy again.

"It's because we never paid him," Lars declared.

"Perhaps," Elskelyn murmured, though privately she doubted it could be so simple.

They left the town and found the thin forest track, much overgrown now, where they had met the boy. But after all these years, there was no sign of him or his fire, no sign even of the clearing where they had been. They kept walking, not knowing what else to do. Vines and whip-like branches twined in front of them, forming a dense screen they had to push through, though the path at their feet remained clear, if narrow. After many hours, however, the way suddenly opened up and they found themselves on a wide dirt trail, like a disused road, dotted here and there with large smooth stones. As they continued walking, the way became even wider and more rocky. Elskelyn kept to the left side, skirting the rocks jumbled in the middle, and Lars strayed to the right. He lagged behind, just as she used to, and she stopped periodically to let him catch up.

Soon she began to see shallow pools beside some of the rocks, and damp earth between them. With excitement, and only a little foreboding, she realized they were following the course of a riverbed. She sensed that they would find the boy before long, that this was where he must live. She stopped and sighted Lars, well behind her now, meandering up the other side, sometimes making slow detours out into the watercourse, not seeming to care about the mud that would be clinging to his boots. Why was he dawdling so? She hurried on, too impatient to wait, knowing he would catch up with her eventually.

By now, the water was a few inches deep—somewhere before the dry part there must be a hole it's dropping into, thought Elskelyn—and up ahead she could see where it became deeper still. She called back to Lars that he should come across while he could, using the stepping stones still clearing the surface. But he was too far back to hear over the rushing water. She tried to say the same thing with signs, pointing at him and then at the stones in a sequence. But he only raised his hand in a slow wave. She saw by the flash of white that he was smiling.

Lars saw Elskelyn gesturing at him from the other side of the dirt road they were walking along. He didn't understand what he was getting at, but he returned her wave, figuring he'd find out soon enough. Everything was like a slow song to him now, a tune he recognized and bobbed his head to. The whole world was Elskelyn and they were dancing a barely moving waltz.

He lost sight of her for a time. But then he came around a bend and saw a sight that made him skip a beat, like a bit of fast jazz dropped into the slow tempo of his walking. Up ahead, a waterfall dropped over a cliff into a dark pool. A squat shape, a small pudgy person, sat on the cliff to the left of the falls, his feet dangling over the edge. Halfway up to him, climbing on rocks slicked by spray, was Elskelyn. The sights seemed familiar, but brightly dangerous. He couldn't place them in his slow-moving thoughts.

"Elskelyn!" he called out, and willed himself to hurry. Despite his fear, though, something slowed him down as if the air were a sludge he was wading through.

Elskelyn, her face rinsed with the intoxicating cold spray, kept climbing. She went faster than she knew she should, almost laughing when her foot or hand slipped on a greasy rock. She had no idea why she was climbing, or why she was climbing so fast; she only knew she had to reach the top.

Lars stopped. He couldn't reach her. His legs were lead. He looked up. She was climbing frantically now,

slipping down and clambering back even faster, as heedless of the drops below her scrabbling feet as of the figure perched above. She became a blur, blending with and then disappearing behind the mist from the falling water.

Panting on the rock face, forced by her stabbing lungs to pause for a moment, Elskelyn looked down and back. She saw Lars frozen still as a statue on the other side of the rushing river that now divided them. His mouth was open, as if he was calling something to her. His hand was at his wrist, as if he meant again to tear off his willow bracelet, perhaps to try to throw it across to her.

Though why, she thought, when her own, next to her eye below a damp rock, was as fresh and gleaming as on the day it was cut?

...strange detours...

Grimus the Miser

David, who was seven, woke up in the middle of the night. He was usually a good sleeper who didn't stir until his mother called him in the morning for breakfast, but tonight his eyes popped open in the dark. He lay face down in his bed, his face turned to his wall of toys and stuffed animals. He felt the fluttery tingles in his stomach that he called the Christmas feeling, as if fireflies had escaped from a jar and were jittering about his insides, winking their lights on and off.

Slowly, to prolong the moment (and so as not to appear greedy), he inched his hand up under his pillow. It was there. His fingertips touched an edge of metal. Once again, the miracle had happened. While he slept, the tooth fairy had taken the tooth he had wrapped in tissue and left behind a bright silver coin. He felt the cool flat smoothness with the pad of his finger, delaying the moment when he would bring it out and clutch it in his fist.

Round. Cool. Flat at first—and then, through the nerves of your fingers, you felt the raised surfaces of the design. Low mounds and curves, the shape of an animal or queen. He felt them with his eyes closed, wondering what it would be like to be blind.

Something was different this time, though. The coin was not cool. Not as cool as it should be, hiding in the dark under his pillow. It felt as if it had just come from a pocket or a hand. Touching it, he realized something was in the room with him.

Don't try to see the fairy, his parents had told him, wagging their fingers. *If she catches you peeking, she won't ever come back again*. They wagged their fingers sternly, but their eyes looked like they were trying not to smile.

David was an obedient boy, and brave—but of course not brave or obedient enough to ignore a creature from another world visiting his room. He turned his head, very slowly, to the right, where he sensed the fairy's presence. He thought she would be small, and bright. A little, glowing pixie hovering in mid-air, or else perched with her wings folded on the edge of his desk or chair.

What he saw made him feel as if he had swallowed a cold huge lump that he couldn't begin to get down his throat.

In the half-lit corner of his bedroom, between his bookcase and the curtained window, stood a huge, hairy creature, so tall that even stooping his head grazed the ceiling. He was great-eyed and shaggy-haired, and black, bristly hairs poked in clumps from his blubbery fat. Under his staring eyes, his mouth was pulpy and wet, gaping to reveal a few pointy teeth with black spaces between them. He was shivering. Shaking all over with a fine tremor.

After the first shock, David felt no fear of the creature; only curiosity. Huge as it was, it looked too miserable to be dangerous. It stared back at David with huge, pleading eyes. Thinking of pictures he had seen in storybooks, David wanted to call it a troll, but it looked more frightened than frightening, and also too big. *Creature* was the only word he could think of.

As he watched, sitting up in bed now with his own eyes wide, David saw the creature vanish. Not all at once, with a pop; and not fading like a ghost. No, the creature vanished in bits and pieces, patches of him shredding away, as if someone had drawn him and was undoing their work with furious eraser rubbings. If vanishing could be painful, this looked painful. The creature's big staring eyes and wet mouth were the last to go.

Curiosity was what made David brave. And it sometimes got him hurt. It had broken his ankle when he wanted to find out what it felt like to jump into a leaf pile from the roof of the garage. *Think. Think first*, his parents told him. And David tried to. But usually he found himself thinking just *after* he had done something, not before.

So, moments after the creature disappeared, David found himself standing where the creature had been. It was strange to see the rumpled bedclothes where he had been sleeping, low bumps and mounds like a flattened shell of himself. He smelled a dirty, sweaty smell, like the laundry hamper before his mother did the washing. It was not strong, and not unpleasant. On the wooden floor, something wet caught the light that came faintly through the parted curtain. It looked like a gob of drool that the creature had slobbered. David touched it with his big toe.

Instantly, he found himself in another place. He was still in a shadowy corner, but he was looking out into a glowing white room with curving walls and a domed roof. It was like the inside of an igloo he had imagined, except that the walls were not smooth but pebbly, as if fitted with hundreds of tiny pointed tiles. The floor was bumpy too. And the light that made the white walls glow came from a bright lamp above a long table, like the bench in a laboratory. The bench and a stool in front of it were the only pieces of furniture in the room. But they were not the only things, or people, in the room.

A very tall, exceptionally thin old man sat on the stool at the long table. Even sitting on the low stool he was much taller than David. He wore a long white coat, and the fingers and wrists emerging from it were so fleshless they looked like wires attached to gray sticks. But they did not look weak, not at all; they looked as strong as a crow's talons. His head was perfectly bald, and glistened as if from a coating of oil. When he turned slightly to one side, David saw a long, sharp nose and a pointed chin. They, too, had a slimy appearance that made David think of Vaseline.

To the thin man's right was a bin heaped with small, white-and-red objects. To his left was an identical bin, also heaped, but with bright silver coins. The man reached for one of the objects from the right-hand bin, and set to work on it with a small metal instrument. David could hear him muttering as he worked: "One for you, one for me. Count one, two. Count two, three." David was used to hearing adults mutter to themselves as they worked, but this muttering made him afraid. There was something of a nursery rhyme in it, like a skipping chant; but the thin man's dry, raspy voice contained no hint of music.

Now David felt a shifting in the shadows beside him and realized he was not alone. He had been so absorbed in watching the strange scene in front of him that he had not seen the creature standing a little distance away, in the shadow of another entranceway, one of many, to this room. The creature darted a glance at him and began making its way across to the workbench. He plodded slowly, as if his joints ached, which perhaps they did, but it was also clear that he was very afraid, and trying his best to make no sound despite his great bulk. Though the dome of the room glittered far above him, he hunched his shoulders, like a guilty thing expecting punishment. When he got close enough to the right-hand bin, he extended a great meaty arm and opened his hairy fist. Something tiny fell onto the pile with a little *chink*.

At the sound, the man at the bench brought his foot up with amazing speed and kicked the creature viciously in the side. The creature grunted, a low yelp; though his side, like the rest of him, was well-padded with flab, already a red spot was brightening where the sharp-toed boot had struck him. He floundered away, with haste that was half-lumbering half-scuttling, through a doorway beyond the bin of coins.

The oily-skinned thin man plucked with his tweezers the new offering from the pile and crouched low over his bench to examine it.

My tooth, David thought. And then was back in his bedroom. With no way to return to the domed white room, no matter how long he stood in the creature's vacated spot in the shadows.

The next day, he behaved as he always had with the other children at school, all of whom were losing their teeth at different rates: showing them his silver coin; grinning to let them see the new space in his mouth, sticking the tip of his tongue through it, forcing air through it with a whistling hiss. But these games, which he had enjoyed only the day before, no longer interested him. (Though he pretended that they did, for nothing gives away a secret faster than a change in interests.) Now, his only interest in missing teeth was in how they might help him reach the trapped creature, whom he had determined to rescue, though he had no idea how.

It was two weeks before his next tooth loosened. On each of those fourteen nights he tried standing in the shadowy corner, and in other spots in his bedroom; but, as he expected, without the tooth under his pillow, they were just ordinary spots in his room.

Then a tooth began to loosen. It was a tooth about halfway back on the upper right side. He felt it shift while he was eating, then worked at it with his tongue and his finger, wiggling it back and forth to loosen it more. Hurried this way, the tooth came out with a little more blood than usual. It pulsed into a tissue for several minutes before it stopped. *Easy, David, easy!* said his mother. *Think, David. Think*, added his father.

He tried to stay awake that night. And then he thought that might spoil everything, and tried to go to sleep. It was difficult to know what to do when you had no idea how things worked. Sometime in the night, he awoke with a start. He stuck his hand under the pillow and found the coin. Cold! He was too late.

He jumped out of bed and went to the corner. There was no creature smell but he saw on the floor a small crust of drool, almost dry. He stuck his big toe on it and twisted it back and forth, like someone stubbing out a cigarette.

He was in the white room. There was no sign of the creature. But the oily-headed thin man was bent over his place at his bench, his face down close to something held in his tweezers, and talking to himself—or to the thing in his hands—in a dry, low voice that was like a mechanical cooing. "You are old enough to understand the ways of exchange. Oh yes, you are. Count it out, and count it in. One for you, and one for me. To and fro, fro and to. One, two; two, three."

It made a kind of sense, and might almost have sounded reasonable, had the cold tick-tock of his voice not sounded completely insane.

While the thin man was preoccupied, David slipped along the wall and through the doorway where the creature had slunk the last time. He found him cowering at the far end of the room. It was amazing how small such a lurking great beast could make himself seem. It was partly his fear, which had him trembling again, but also the fact that the ceiling in his room was very low, and he had to bend low and hunch his head between his shoulders. Standing on tiptoe, David came up almost to the creature's chin.

"Who are you?" David whispered, glancing over his shoulder at the room he had left.

The creature shivered as if a freezer door had opened, and shook his head violently.

"What's your name?" David whispered again.

With great moist eyes staring in fright, the creature tried to answer. It revolved its slobbery lips, and David saw behind them brown-black jagged stumps—not holes but rather broken teeth, bits of teeth, as if his mouth had been smashed in—and behind these, a raw meaty thing wagging back and forth. This, David realized with horror, was what remained of the creature's tongue.

After much effort, he made a sound, which David heard as no more than a wet grunt. But he tried again, and then again; and either he got better at making the sound, or David got better at hearing it, for finally he heard, thickly but clearly, "Grimus."

"Grimus? That's you?"

The creature trembled and shook his head again. With jerks of his shaggy head at the lighted room beyond David, he said, "Grimus. Grimus . . . come. Grimus . . . do."

And then David understood that Grimus was the creature's tormentor, the thin man bent over his bench between his bins. The creature delivered his coins for him, and brought back his teeth; and spent the rest of his time in fear, dodging kicks. David was more determined than ever to help the creature, though he still had no idea how.

Go, go, the creature seemed to be saying now, with shooing motions of his paw-like hands; and David remembered that his time in this place was short, and would end abruptly.

He tried to leave the creature with some comfort. "I'll come back," he whispered. But the creature was no longer listening. Shaking its head from side to side, it was making fast gurgling sounds, as if trying to explain something quickly. But David could make no sense of it, and had to go.

He crept out of the creature's shadowy lair. When he reached the doorway, he put his hand out to the wall, wanting to check that Grimus was busy before he stole across behind him. The wall felt pebbly, like a tile wall, but also sharp. Looking closely, he saw that it was made of rows and rows of tiny white teeth, points facing outward.

The next thing he saw was his bed with its rumpled covers.

A few days later, his next tooth loosened. He worked it free and stanched the blood. But a terrible thing happened. He fell into such a deep sleep that when he woke up, morning light was coming through the curtains and the coin under his pillow was stone cold. He felt ashamed at the thought of the creature standing in his corner waiting helplessly for him to follow. He stood in the corner for a long time, though he knew it was hopeless, and then he went down to breakfast with his parents.

By the end of the long, boring day at school, he had worked out a plan.

The only problem was, the plan needed a loose tooth, and he didn't have one. Pressing hard against each of his remaining teeth, he couldn't make one budge. He wasn't sure he even had a baby tooth left. His mother thought he might be done with them. But he found a tooth on the lower left that, if not a baby tooth, was at least small, and began pressing on it from either side with his forefinger. He pressed as hard as he could stand, until tears came to his eyes. And then he took a little rest. And then he pressed again.

The tooth was solid. It took several hours of presses before it moved even a little. And then two more days before it went from the slowly side-to-side shifting stage to looser wiggling. Smears of blood came away on his fingers when he pressed. It hurt a lot. When it felt almost loose enough to give way, David left it alone until that night.

Once his mother had tucked him in, he waited until he heard his parents go to bed. Then, quietly, he got dressed again and sat on the edge of his bed. He pushed at the tooth until it gave a final lurch, almost free; a thick wad of blood spurted into the tissue he had ready, some of the blood going thickly down his throat. He went to the shadowy corner where he had first seen the creature. Taking a deep breath because he knew how much it would hurt, he jabbed at the tooth with his thumb, hard, and knocked it out of its socket.

Nothing happened for a few seconds. His mouth hurt terribly, and the tissue was soaked with blood. David wasn't sure what was supposed to happen. His plan had never been very detailed. All he knew was that he had to help the creature, and the only way he could think of to do that was to break the sequence the

creature was trapped in: baby tooth falls out, goes under pillow, gets traded for a coin, gets returned to Grimus. As long as things happened that way, David didn't see any hope for the creature. Perhaps with a tooth pushed out before its time, and no coin involved, no sleeping child—maybe, somehow, they could get the jump on Grimus and his system.

David felt a scratchy sensation in his legs, as if wool was being rubbed against them, and looked down to see them disappearing, as the creature's legs had disappeared that first time. And then he saw the same thing happen to one of his hands. A scratchy rubbing went down it, taking a piece away, and then another scratchy rubbing took another piece. It was a slow and uncomfortable way to vanish, not at all like the neat pop or wink of cartoons. He was glad when the scratchy rubbing started in places around his head; they felt worst of all, but they meant it would soon be over.

It was. He was standing in the shadowy entranceway where he had first seen the white domed room made of children's teeth. Grimus was on his stool at his bench, working with his tweezers, muttering to himself. Near him, on the floor beside the tooth bin, the creature sat, his great legs splayed sloppily, with a bucket of water between them in which he was washing teeth, taking a bloody fresh one from the bin and working it clumsily between his fingers in the water. Then he would lay it on a towel on the edge of the bench. Grimus reached over with his tweezers and took the cleaned tooth into his workspace. From time to time, he kicked with his boot at the creature beside him, hitting him in the side, on the arm, or, once, on the side of the face. Sometimes the creature grunted at these blows, flinching away, but sometimes he didn't react at all. Just absorbed it and went on working over his bucket.

David waited a long time while this work and punishment went on. Suddenly, Grimus stared off into space above his workbench, staring into the wall of white teeth facing him, and his muttering became excited. David knew that somewhere a child had gone to sleep with a tooth under its pillow. Grimus swore and kicked at the creature, which was already getting clumsily to its feet. It lumbered toward David, but when it saw him, its eyes went huge with fear, and it veered into its room.

David crept along the wall after it. Grimus was too excited to notice, clasping and unclasping his hands with a horrid washing motion and muttering intensely all the while.

When David stood in front of the creature, he opened his hand on the large tooth he was holding. In the instant the creature saw the fresh white tooth with its long bloody root, a remarkable transformation occurred. It occurred in a single moment, with none of the scratchy rubbings of transition that David and the creature were both familiar with.

In front of David stood no troll-like creature, flabby and hairy, but a slim, dark-haired boy only a few years older and a little taller than himself. He wore a close-fitting vest and leggings, and a thin leather belt around his waist with a sheath on his right hip. From this, with a practiced motion, he drew a short knife. As he did so, he put his finger up in front of his lips, signing *Shhh*. David watched all this with his mouth open in shock. Nothing about the slim boy or his quick and purposeful motions bore the slightest resemblance to the shambling, pathetic giant of a few seconds before. Though the boy had signed for silence, David had no doubt that he could speak well, and he hoped that he would get a chance to hear him.

The boy went swiftly and silently to the door, David following close behind. The boy approached Grimus at his bench. At the last moment, Grimus sensed him and turned. He uttered a shriek of outrage and then began babbling uncontrollably, as if his former mutterings had all joined together and risen to a pitch of panic, which sounded to David's ears like a mixture of cats wailing in a sack and alarm clocks going off.

The boy raised his knife, which glinted in the light. Grimus shrieked again, and dropped to the floor, where he became a lizard-like creature, white and gray, with a smooth head, and slimy all over as if covered with glue. He scuttled away across the floor of teeth. But the boy jumped ahead of him, crouched down, and cut him in half. Each half quivered, then grew legs and scuttled on in different directions, a little more slowly than before. This, too, the boy was prepared for. He sliced the lizard on his right in half, and then flipped the knife into his left hand and severed the lizard on that side. Again the remnants quivered, grew legs, and tried to escape—but it took a second longer, and the lizards were smaller than before.

Working quickly with his knife, slicing it down with unerring swiftness, the boy dispatched the multiplying selves of Grimus, which grew in number as they shrank in size and power—until, finally, he had exhausted his power to divide himself. What was left in the glowing white room were dozens of tiny, slow-moving lizards, so small they resembled bugs, and so weakened that they milled about in a confused way, crawling here and there over the floor.

"Now kill them," said the boy, in a voice as clear as anyone's. "Every one." And he showed David how, with a stamp of his heel on the lizard-thing closest to him.

It took David and the boy some time to kill all of the slowly scuttling parts of Grimus. The bug-like lizards crunched unpleasantly underfoot, but as they did so, that patch of tooth-floor changed to normal-looking pebbles, like those you might find on a beach. Some of the Grimus-bugs crawled up the walls, and it was even more unpleasant to crush them under one's hand. But the walls, too, gradually turned to the rock bits on the sides of a cave, with bits of moss and earth between them.

Finally, when all the dirty work had been done, the boy and David were sitting in a pleasant cave, on a stone-and-dirt floor. Grimus's terrible bench was only a ledge of rock, long and straight, and the light above it was a hole in the cave through which the moon shone. Even the creature's washing bucket had been transformed, into a little pool of water fed by tricklings down a mossy patch on the roof of the cave. As they lay there, the boy recounted to David the story of the spell Grimus had placed him under, which had robbed him of his speech and proper shape and condemned him to serve Grimus in his miserly eternal exchange of teeth for silver coins. Only one thing could save him, which Grimus had told him with a laugh, not expecting it could ever occur. He could be rescued—which Grimus forbade him ever to reveal, and then made double sure by cutting out his tongue—only if a child offered him a tooth of its own free will, expecting nothing in return. That would release him from Grimus's spell.

Listening to this, David felt himself becoming sleepy. As interesting as the boy's story was, and as pleasant as it was to hear him tell it in his clear strong voice, David was up far, far past his normal bedtime; it was near the end of a long night; and though the ground was hard, he had made himself comfortable lying with his head on his bent arm. The one thing he wanted to ask the boy, while he still had the power to remain in this place, was whether there was such a thing as fairies and whether he himself, the boy, was one or of another race entirely, and he was waiting for a place in the boy's story where he could interrupt not too rudely—

—when he realized he had missed his chance, he was back in his own bed, in his own room, and the faint sounds he heard in the distance where those of his mother and father stirring in the kitchen downstairs.

The King's Huntsman

In a distant land, a powerful king offered the following terms to anyone who would wrestle him. The contestant must wager his life, but if he prevailed in the match, the king would reward him with one of his prize horses and a huge bag of gold. Though the king's wrestling skill was legendary, many strong men were desperate or noble enough to try him at his terms. Most lost quickly; a few pushed the king hard; one or two tested him to his limit—but in the end, all climbed the steps to the scaffold which stood directly behind the wrestling area.

After a few years, only vagrants and lunatics were willing to risk their lives against the king. And the king, who was as just as he was proud, would not accept such hopeless challenges.

That is why at first he declined when word reached his ears that a newcomer in town, a poor soldier, wished to try him. The soldier—so the king's attendants reported—was of no rank or distinction, not old but not quite young, and of middling stature. When the newcomer persisted in his challenge, the king had him brought to court.

"Do you know who and what you will be fighting for?" the king asked the soldier, who looked as unremarkable as his courtiers had described.

"I will be fighting you for my life, which is all I have," said the soldier, returning the king's gaze steadily.

"And why do you think you can win where so many others have lost?" asked the king.

"For the reason I already gave," said the soldier.

And the king, who thought that if the soldier was insane it was at least in a way that interested him, ordered the preparations for the match. The executioner was summoned. Courtiers and their ladies packed the viewing stands. The two contestants stripped to fight. The match was the longest and fiercest anyone had witnessed, filled with pins and falls and close calls on both sides, but in the end the court saw what it had learned to think impossible: the king pinned helplessly, signalling defeat with a grim nod.

That evening, the king, who was as magnanimous as he was just, invited the victorious soldier to a banquet in his honour. He seated him beside him and they ate and drank and watched the entertainments. As the

evening drew to a close, the king offered to make the soldier one of his knights and, further, to give him one of his own daughters in marriage.

The soldier lowered his head and took his time answering, hesitating so long that those listening (while pretending not to) shifted nervously in their seats.

"Thank you," said the soldier, raising his eyes at last, "but soldier has proved rank enough for me. And your daughter deserves better than a common man. Even," he added, "one with a fine horse and a bag of gold."

The king's face hardened with displeasure, for he was as vain as he was magnanimous, but he acknowledged the soldier's wishes with a nod. That night, though, the king twisted in his bed, tossing in and out of a troubled sleep. In the morning, as the soldier was preparing to depart, the king stood with him at a window overlooking the courtyard where the king's best black stallion was being loaded with a leather bag bulging with gold.

"You're obviously a gambler," said the king casually, for he was as sly as he was vain, "so I wonder if you would be interested in one more small wager."

When the soldier said he might be, the king took him to another window overlooking a small weedy plot. On one side of it stood a goose and a goat in a pen; on the other, an old man dozed on a bench.

"I will send you away with double your winnings," said the king, "if you will agree to let my huntsman pursue you. If he catches you, you will owe him your head."

"I will need to see this huntsman you are betting on," said the soldier, whom a perilous life had taught to be prudent as well as bold, depending on the circumstances.

The king gestured down at the old man on the bench.

The soldier smiled; the king did not. And the soldier, after a pause of consideration, agreed.

Immediately, the king called down for a goose for supper. And the old man, without looking up at his master's voice, lifted himself slowly from his bench and hobbled across the weedy yard. It seemed to take him half the morning to shuffle the short distance. And the soldier, though he watched without expression, felt alarm at the sight of the figure's scanty gray hair and threadbare gray cloak; for he knew the strength and cunning in the man he had bested the night before, who would surrender nothing easily. When the old man finally reached the animal pen, something flashed in his hand—so fast the soldier never knew if it was an axe or a sword—and the goose's head was lying on the ground a full second before its body could fall and join it.

"He is as relentless as he is merciless," said the king in a musing voice. "Go wherever you like. He is an expert tracker. All he needs is one look at your back, which I will give him when you go."

With a curt nod, the king turned to leave. After a few steps, however, he turned back to say one thing more.

"There is one way to evade him, but no one has ever discovered it. You've given no sign of needing my help, so I'm sure you don't want it now." He smiled coldly. "Until I see you again."

And he strode away down the corridor of his castle.

TROTTING AWAY on the black horse, the soldier felt a cold prickling between his shoulders at the thought of the old huntsman watching him. Watching and memorizing. As soon as he was out of sight of the castle, he kicked the horse into a hard gallop. Despite the heavy bags of gold hanging from the saddle, the black horse fairly flew over the ground, and the soldier drove him until his flanks were frothing. Even so, when he finally let up, he turned with his heart in his throat, expecting to see the old huntsman with his terrible blade right behind him. But of course the road was empty. He laughed out loud at his own foolishness, and led the horse to a stream for a good long drink and rest.

The soldier had been in too many dire battles to let the deft butchery of a goose dismay him for long. The king had tried a black joke at the end, that was all. Unhappy at losing, he had hoped for some slight revenge: planting a seed of fear by trickery where he had failed to plant one in the wrestling ring.

Still, to be prudent, the soldier urged the black horse along the road as hard as he dared, stopping only for the briefest and most necessary rests, riding each day until nightfall and then, after snatching a few hours sleep at an inn, setting off at dawn again. After a few such days, he stopped earlier one afternoon. At this rate he would soon turn the magnificent horse into a broken-down nag. He ordered himself dinner and wine.

How many weeks, he thought, would it take a strong walker to cover the ground I've ridden in these days? (Even assuming he knew the way, for the soldier had changed course often, especially at first.) How many months—or years—would it take a hobbling, shuffling old man?

He smiled into his cup, finished the rest of the wine, and before bed visited the stallion to see how he'd enjoyed the oat mash he'd ordered him.

Finally, he relaxed, and let his good fortune surround him like the quilt on the inn's best bed.

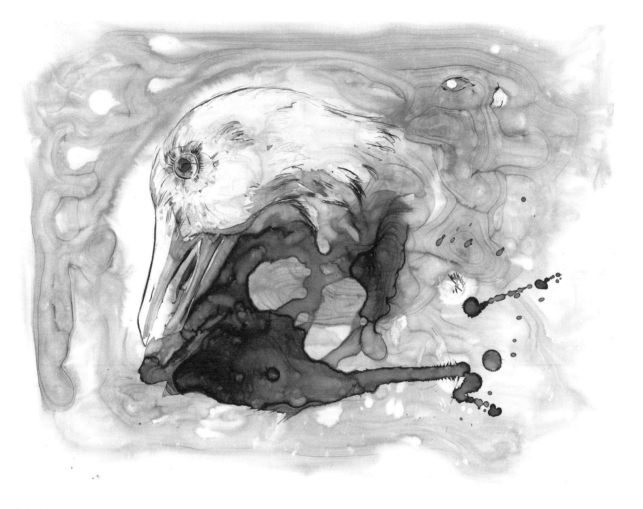

And then, in the instant just before sleep, he saw the bent gray figure, whom he had endowed with no need to sleep, limping towards him through the dark. Making up a little ground, pace by slow pace, while his quarry slept.

And he saw the eye of the goose, open and unsurprised, staring up from the ground.

IN THIS WAY the king had his revenge. It was a subtle revenge, to be sure: nothing like being thrown to the ground and pinned before one's astonished (and no doubt secretly delighted) subjects, as he himself had endured. And, over time, the image of the pursuing huntsman worked less powerfully on the soldier's mind. He was still not quite old, and he had two bags of gold with which to distract himself. Still, he moved around a lot, even for a wealthy bachelor. He told himself that he had always been restless, and now he had the means to satisfy those urges. Hadn't the dread of settling driven him into the soldiering life to begin with? Yet—he had slept better as a soldier. His hand had been steadier. Even the night before a battle, it had been.

The scene of the huntsman and goose in the weedy courtyard dwindled in his thoughts to the echo of a scene. And then the echo of the echo of a scene. And then the echo of the echo of an echo . . . —without ever, even for a moment, getting so faint that he forgot it entirely.

Certain dull shades of gray wool had the power to startle him, especially if he turned and saw them close behind him.

He was uncomfortable standing with his back to a roadway, or even to a room, and he felt most relaxed with a wall behind his shoulders, clear sightlines ahead.

Foolishness! Foolishness! he chided himself. And laughed at himself, and felt some moments of relief. And then some thought such as *Is it foolishness for a sparrow to glance around constantly?*—or another like it—would come creeping back into his brain.

He is relentless.

An old man, a hunter, slowly hobbling after his quarry.

A goose head, staring.

HE MARRIED at forty. Something he had put off for a long time, despite a rich bachelor's many opportunities, for fear of bringing another into his predicament. But he fell in love, and that decided it. It decided it in the blind, unreasoning way love decides everything. He had bought businesses along the way with his money, and these supplied enough income that he didn't need to touch what remained of the king's gold. His wife, who was much younger than he, loved to travel, so for a few years they were happy moving about seeing the world, without him having to believe that he was always running *away*. It was when she said that she wanted them to buy a house and have a child while she was still young enough—that was the moment when the fear returned, or reminded him with a dull throb that it had never left. But the throb passed, and all was well again. There was even a busy spell, during the flurry of purchasing the house and settling into it, when he became sure that he was done for good with limping gray huntsmen and goose heads. The echo was that faint.

And then, one night in bed, his wife sleeping beside him, he caught himself calculating how vast the distances were, how many long and twisting roads lay between their bedroom and the wrestling king's castle. It was an episode long ago, in a far country.

And then he thought, he remembered, that there is no road—no distance—not abolished by a huntsman willing to hobble down it forever.

Their child was born. A girl. She grew and was healthy. And the house was happy—not perfectly so, for what house is?—but too happy to be much marred by the father's nervous habit of going about rooms peering out of windows; or of visiting several times a day his old black horse, grown white in the muzzle —standing patting it while they faced the road together, in the manner of two old campaigners having a conference.

He didn't tell his wife his secret. Half the time it was a joke too ludicrous to admit; the other half, a horror too monstrous to burden her with. There was no in-between.

Joy and dread were two sides of the same instant. Joy was watching his daughter pick one of the flowers she loved to find in the yard; watching his wife's face as she brought it to them. Dread, which came hard after, was a goose with its neck stretched in the sun.

He left when his daughter was ten. Which, he thought, looking at his wife's and daughter's faces on their last morning together, was—even at the slowest rate of hobbling—at least nine years too late. Nine years of risk too long.

(Curiously, in all this time, during which he himself was getting old, not once did it occur to him that the huntsman might die. Something deathless was in the flash of his steel. And he only very seldom nursed the hope that his steps might slow further and his skills decline. What is the difference between steel flashing at lightning or at half-lightning speed?)

He took nothing with him but the clothes on his back. His wife and child had need of the rest of the gold. And he would not need money for what he meant to do. And, too, he had always had a lurking suspicion, a fantasy perhaps, that the king's revenge would end if he no longer enjoyed the money he had taken from him.

For the same reason he did not visit the black horse to say goodbye.

Let's turn and git 'em. It had been the motto of a foolish, much-loved friend the soldier had served with long ago. Brave in any forward action, he could not endure the helplessness of retreat. Always, when they were on the run, he had to turn and find the ones pursuing them in the darkness. He had lived longer than anyone expected, finally dying in one of his hopeless charges shortly before the soldier found his way to the wrestler king's court. And the soldier thought of him now because he had finally reached the same limit of nerves: he would rather run into the arms of certain death than spend a single minute more evading it.

There is one way to evade him . . . .

And one way not to, thought the soldier. And that is the way for me.

[146]

It seemed illogical to go to meet a tracker, whose job it is to be always behind you, tracing your signs and footsteps. But it was the absoluteness of the king's confidence in his man—*He is relentless . . . He is an expert tracker*—that assured the soldier that his plan would work. That plus his absolute fatigue at living on the run: nothing exhausts so thoroughly as fear, and nothing breeds faith in success like exhaustion, which has no energy left to fail with.

Thus the soldier started retracing the paths of his life that led back towards the castle. Walking back along the many criss-crossing strands he had laid across the world, undoing his journey, certain that if he did so long enough and carefully enough, he would meet the one limping to find him.

It took years. He got sick often, sometimes for months at a time, as a result of his beggar's diet and constant walking—and, by this time, of his age. Once, he had to hole up for over a year with a woman and her children, depending in his helplessness on their charity. It was like a second married life, one in a dream. The woman wept when he left, and so did he. He no longer thought of such stationary times as dangerous, only wasteful. They seemed like lives athwart his life, set outside and at a slant to it.

Whenever he got underway again, he marvelled anew at the devious branching labyrinth he had constructed for the huntsman. It wasn't a maze that he would have any trouble negotiating—but, certainly, it would take time. Time for anybody. It was always a question of time . . . only of that, he muttered to himself, mumbling aloud in the way that all solitaries eventually acquire.

He met the huntsman on a stretch of unremarkable road, mid-morning. The event had no drama. Events too long prepared for never do.

He walked towards him, not quickly and not slowly. Just as he had promised himself to do. (Though also, with age and illness, his former soldier's stride had decayed and taken on aspects of the huntsman's limping shuffle.)

The approaching figure looked as he remembered: bent, thin, gray-clad. Face lowered to watch the ground —for signs? or just for footing?

He had never had more than a quick general impression of the huntsman, a few solid facts bundled together with reams of fantasy and supposition.

They were not far apart now. Why did the huntsman not raise his face at footsteps he must hear approaching? Because he was too intent on his quarry to be distracted? Or because, already aware of that

quarry with a huntsman's infallible instincts, he was preparing the steel beneath his sleeve?

Neck stretched like a goose, the soldier reminded himself, *eyes open like a man*.

Ten paces . . . then five . . . then two separated them. One.

The huntsman looked up: clear gray eyes in a deeply lined face.

The huntsman glanced at him and passed by.

In that instant the soldier's world slid out from under him. It spun and tipped on its side, the way it had once in a battle when an unexpected blow had sent him to the ground and for strange instants screaming men had become reeling wisps of cloud.

All he needs is one look at your back . . . .

The look at one who will be forever fleeing. The one sight he will never need to learn is the sight of your face, coming to meet him.

Of course.

The soldier turned and saw that the shuffling huntsman was gone. The road was long and level; he had not disappeared along it. He was gone.

He stood for a while in the empty road, wanting to laugh, feeling that was called for, but able only to manage deep, aching breaths, the ribcage loosening its iron hoops after years of tension. These breaths felt like laughter, and for a time he gave himself fully to them, bent over in the road like a runner after a race, before starting on the way back to find what might remain of his family.

The Spigot

A painter broken by bad luck and bad habits sat in an alley with his back to a brick wall. In another the posture might have betokened despair, but with this painter it was closer to the opposite: a prayer for hope—a hope for hope—in the sort of place that had always cheered him most.

His most successful exhibition, many years before, had been a showing of paintings of derelict places and things entitled "Waste Spaces." A friend of his, a writer, had composed a poem for the catalogue catching the painter's predilections: *Waste spaces, alleys, vacant lots . . . .*

The show had been a modest success by his standards. A dozen people had come to the opening, sampling the cheese platters and wine. Two small views of glass shards on asphalt had sold. Over the three week run, signatures, some with appreciative comments, had filled four pages of the gallery's Guest Book.

There had even been a published review, his first. But when the review spoke of "ironic commentary," the painter was dismayed. He felt as if he were seeing himself in a funhouse mirror. How could anyone find irony in the sheer joy he took in his subjects, in all the luscious hues and textures of neglect? Or find commentary in the exuberance with which he tried to render that joy on canvas?

The show was only a minor event some twenty years before, but the painter dated the start of his decline from it.

Now, after losing family, friends and the roof over his head, he had lost the one thing he had managed to keep through all that tumult: his art.

What can I do? he murmured in the alley. Who will tell me?

I'm all ears, said a voice to his side. It seemed to come from the vicinity of a rusty iron spigot protruding from the old bricks of the wall.

Who are you?

An oracle.

The painter winced. An oracle? Then why aren't people lined up around the block to consult you?

I think you can answer that one for yourself.

The painter looked at the spigot in the brick wall. The voice was of indeterminate gender—it could be a low woman's voice, or a high man's voice. Such uncertainty fit with oracles, he seemed to recall. The voice also seemed to be quirky, casual, a bit smart-ass. Did that fit with the oracle picture, too? He couldn't remember.

How can I trust what you say? he asked.

I don't know. It sounded like *I don't care. Try me on some questions and see how I do.*

All right, then. What will I do tonight?

Something you should have done yesterday, and something that should wait until tomorrow.

The painter asked, after a hesitation, When will I die?

When news of the event catches up to you.

What am I thinking at this moment?

Wondering if I can be blamed on drugs or madness, in which case you could ignore me.

The painter put his face in his hands, but did not weep. Nor did he feel like weeping, a fact that surprised him a little. Mainly, he felt thirsty.

No one has bothered to shut me off.

He turned the vaguely star-shaped knob above the spigot. Creaks and gurgles came from far away, behind the brick. The painter cupped his palms and put them below the spigot. Finally, a few rust flakes fell out, carried by a trickle of dusty, taffy-coloured water. The water with its orange-black grains and flakes of rust drifted and swayed in a slow swirl above the pale flesh of his palms with their black and white paint stains.

It all formed a striking composition, a deep and depthless beauty in his hands.

Acknowledgements

Mike Barnes thanks the Ontario Arts Council for Writers' Reserve grants which furthered *The Reasonable Ogre*.

Segbingway would like to thank Dan Wells for taking on an unusual and complicated project, and Dennis Priebe for his taste and clarity in helping to shape the book. Segbingway is also grateful to family and friends for their support over the years. In particular to Thomas and Quentin, for their limitless imaginations.

About the Author

Mike Barnes is the author of seven previous books: the novels *Catalogue Raisonné* and *The Syllabus*, the short-fiction collections *Aquarium* (winner of the 1999 Danuta Gleed Award) and *Contrary Angel*, the poetry collections *Calm Jazz Sea* and *A Thaw Foretold*, and *The Lily Pond: A Memoir of Madness, Memory, Myth, and Metamorphosis*. Born in Minnesota, a joint U.S.-Canadian citizen, Mike lives and writes in Toronto.

About the Illustrator

Segbingway is an artist who lives in Toronto.

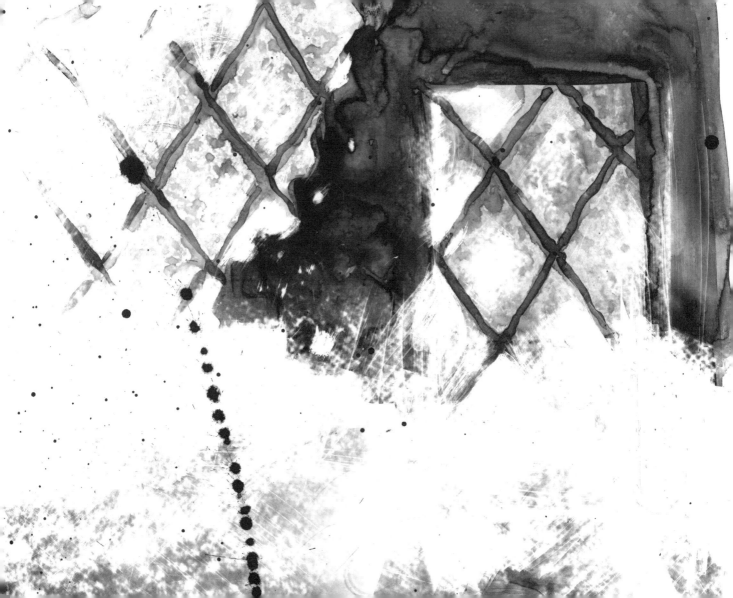

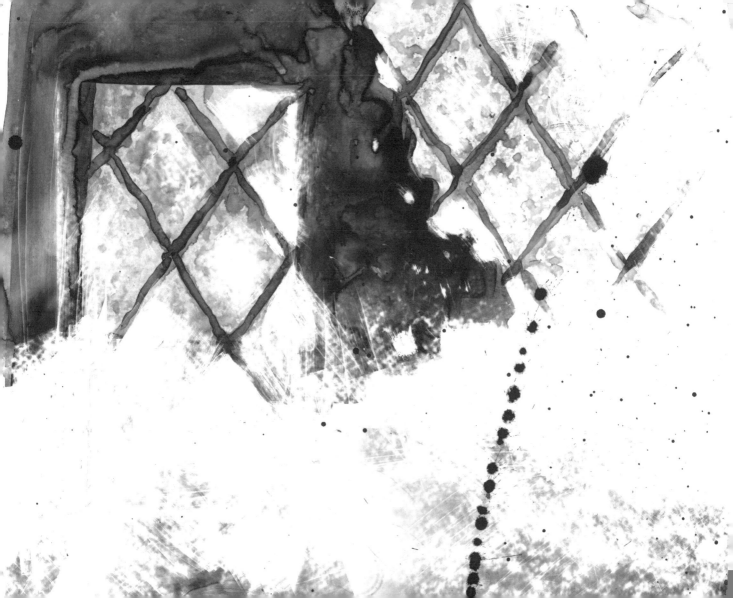